MAXZYNE
and the
OLD HORSE
THEATRE

MAXZYNE
and the
OLD HORSE THEATRE

CAROLINE LEE

Illustrated by Rebecca Robinson

Maxzyne and the Old Horse Theatre
Copyright © 2020 by Caroline Lee

Pendant Press LLC
Delray Beach, Florida

Visit us on the web! www.maxzyne.com
Teaching tools for educators and librarians: www.maxzyne.com/educators/

ISBN: 978-0-9906617-3-3
eISBN: 978-0-9906617-4-0

Cover art and interior illustrations by Rebecca Robinson
Book design by GKS Creative

Publisher's Cataloging-In-Publication Data
(Prepared by The Donohue Group, Inc.)

Names: Lee, Caroline, 1960- author. | Robinson, Rebecca, 2003- illustrator.
Title: Maxzyne and the Old Horse Theatre / Caroline Lee ; illustrated by Rebecca Robinson.
Description: Delray Beach, Florida : Pendant Press LLC, [2020] | Series: [Maxzyne adventure series] ; [2] | Summary: With the help of Rico, an immigrant boy who rides horses in the nearby historic theater, Maxzyne tries to save a runaway horse and carriage before the Chicago Festival of Lights parade.
Identifiers: ISBN 9780990661733 | ISBN 9780990661740 (ebook)
Subjects: LCSH: Schoolgirls--Illinois--Chicago--Juvenile fiction. | Horses--Illinois--Chicago--Juvenile fiction. | Rescues--Illinois--Chicago--Juvenile fiction. | Immigrant children--Illinois--Chicago--Juvenile fiction. | Civics--Juvenile fiction. | Political participation--Juvenile fiction. | Animal rights--Illinois--Chicago--Juvenile fiction. | CYAC: Schoolgirls--Illinois--Chicago--Fiction. | Horses--Illinois--Chicago--Fiction. | Rescues--Illinois--Chicago--Fiction. | Immigrant children--Illinois--Chicago--Fiction. | Civics--Fiction. | Political participation--Fiction. | Animal rights--Illinois--Chicago--Fiction.
Classification: LCC PZ7.1.L39488 Mao 2020 (print) | LCC PZ7.1.L39488 (ebook) | DDC [Fic]--dc23

3-4-20

For Erika

Jillian,
May you find the
magic in everyday
moments — just like
Maxzyne.

Caroline Lee

Contents

1

The Sketch of Doom

THE DOOR TO CLASSROOM 108 closes behind Maxzyne Merriweather with a soft whoosh of air. *It's so weird that school could ever be this quiet.* Her stomach trembles as she looks up and down the hall lined with lockers. Empty. If only the paper in her hand were an ordinary restroom pass. She blinks, willing the page to disappear, but it stays in her shaking hand. There is no denying the awful reason for her early dismissal from Miss Garrett's weekly music class. She sighs, twisting the offending piece of paper. Shiny lead-pencil markings smudge her fingers. *No way it's my fault!* She bites her bottom lip, but her conscience pricks. *Okay, well, yes, it is my sketch. What a rookie mistake,* she chides herself.

But there's a five-syllable word for this problem. Her slim brown fingers automatically count the syllable beats as she whispers, "Ex-ten-u-a-ting circumstances."

She glares at her gray-tinged fingers. Nope. She won't get off easy by making excuses. Besides, her punishment will be a lot worse than having to memorize a big vocabulary word. That's her parents' usual form of discipline for doing something wrong. Her lunch curdles in her stomach. What will they do now that she's been sent to the principal's office?

One problem at a time, she reminds herself. That's what her dad always says. Especially when he gets home after a crazy day at work and her mother insists he help his daughter with her science project before dinner. Although this is much worse than a last-minute school deadline. Last-minute on her end, of course. Last-minute because she's been playing with her new kaleidoscopic computer program, drawing stuff instead of doing homework. But who wouldn't choose to discover the latest in anime rather than write a report about the organization and structure of ant colonies? Puh-leez. Except the drawing part, of course. Maxzyne always gets extra credit for her artwork. Except today. She swallows hard and trudges toward the principal's office. *How do I explain the sketch?* she worries.

If only she hadn't drawn the music teacher quite so realistically. She stops walking and stares at the wrinkled page torn from her spiral notebook. Nope. The evidence is right there in #2 pencil, with her bold signature scrawled underneath. What was she thinking, signing it? Her shoulders sag and her stomach does an anxious somersault. Maybe she's coming down with something. She quickly puts her hand on her forehead, willing a fever to brew. *Hey! Maybe I can claim "temporary temperature insanity."* Unfortunately, her forehead remains cool to the touch. No such luck.

"Sometimes you're such a show-off, Maxzyne!" she groans. Her finger traces the familiar lines on the sketch. Yes, it really is their chubby teacher's goofy smile. That's also her bulky turtleneck and dimpled knees peeking beneath a short plaid skirt. She glares at the portrait. Her mother warned her about doodling in class. Absolutely *anyone* would recognize Miss Garrett as she sings and strums that ghastly autoharp. "I mean, really—who plays the autoharp anyway?" the eleven year old huffs under her breath. Miss Garrett should expect to see herself in a cartoon. Doesn't she know how silly she looks? So uncool. Especially those tiny feet with double-wide jelly calves squeezed into fuzzy sheepskin boots. Feet that constantly tap to the beat of those ancient folk songs she makes students sing. Ble—eccch!

If only she hadn't shown Courtney Crowder the sketch. That was the beginning of the end, she recalls. *It was supposed to be a joke.* The cartoon was just something to distract them—okay, herself—from Miss Garrett's dopey songs. Her lip curls to one side as her conscience pricks again. *Just admit it . . . you were showing off again.* She scowls, remembering how the joke ended up being on her.

All because Courtney grabbed the sketch and scribbled a mean caption underneath: *Miss G's Application for American Superstar.* "Give it back," Maxzyne had begged, mouthing the words behind her spiral notebook while keeping one eye on Miss Garrett. With a sly grin and nonchalant flip of her blonde-streaked ponytail, Courtney ignored her pleas. Instead, she leaned forward to poke Frances Cooper on the shoulder. An accomplished note passer, Frances didn't even turn around. Cool as a cucumber, she smoothed her long wavy hair behind one ear. Maxzyne watched her classmate rest her rhinestone-studded fingers on the back of her neck. *Voila!* The sketch dropped into her waiting fingers. Frances pretended to cough, bringing her hand toward her mouth. Then she smiled straight at their teacher and dropped the note into her lap, quickly unfolding it. Her shoulders shook with laugher as she viewed the sketch with Courtney's caption scrawled on it. Seconds later, she passed it on as Maxzyne's heart fluttered in her chest. She held her breath, fearing disaster as the sketch moved forward along the row of bored students.

Her eyes darted sideways, daring to see if Miss Garrett noticed. For that moment, at least, their teacher was oblivious. She strummed the autoharp, her voice wobbling toward the high notes of a folksy chorus. For a second or two, Miss Garrett's eyes closed, the freckles on her nose crinkling as she strained her vocal cords. The tendons in her pale neck knotted alarmingly the louder she sang. Maxzyne joined in, desperately hoping the teacher wouldn't notice that nearly everyone had stopped singing. Around her, the sketch continued from desk to desk, each time earning a snicker from her classmates. *Why didn't I just stick to drawing the carriage horses I see sometimes outside the classroom window?* she groaned silently. She glanced out the window but didn't see any carriage horses carrying tourists through the historic neighborhood at the moment.

Meanwhile, the sketch was on the move. She agonized while two rows over, Ben Williams added a "five thumbs down" rating. Not to be outdone, Matt Spencer sketched hairy stubble on their teacher's round white legs. Finally, a hippie-era headband decorated with peace signs was added to Miss Garrett's frizzy red hair by a snickering Dave Robinson. Worse, the song ended just as the altered drawing returned to Maxzyne. Too late, the *real* Miss Garrett sensed something was up. She looked around the room, puzzled by the snorts of laughter coming from the boys. Her eyes narrowed as she frowned, her plump cheeks growing pink.

With an ominous prickle of dread, Maxzyne recognized that universal look adults sometimes get. The desperate-but-dazed look that crosses over their face once they realize they are no longer in charge. *Uh-oh. Here it comes.* The Geek Squad "straight-A's" sitting in the front row turned around and stared at her. Worse, a pencil eraser sailed through the air and hit her on the shoulder, bouncing off her desk.

Before Maxzyne could hide the sketch, Miss Garrett was beside her. The angry teacher snatched the cartoon. Her lipsticked mouth opened and closed like a fish sucking algae from the green glass windows at Shedd Aquarium. Darker streaks of pink crept from her cheeks and down her neck, disappearing into the loose folds of her nubby blue-striped turtleneck. The other students held their breath, thrilled by the spectacle. Miss Garrett flicked her tongue and then somehow managed to stretch her lips into a false smile.

Maxzyne slumped even lower in her seat. For once, she dreaded the spotlight. The smell of Miss Garrett's lavender body lotion was wafting in waves from her warm, flushed skin. *Gee, isn't lavender supposed to be calming? Maybe she won't get so mad after all.*

"You'll need to show this to the principal, Miss Merriweather," the teacher ordered in a crisp, take-no-prisoners voice. With both hands on her hips, Miss Garrett glared up and down the desk rows. None of the students lifted their eyes to meet her gaze. Annoyed, she clapped her hands for attention. "Class, unless someone wants to join Maxzyne, let's get back to the *musical arts*, shall we?" She cleared her throat and marched back to her autoharp at the front of the classroom.

There was the scrape of metal chair legs on tile as Maxzyne pushed away from the desk. With shaking hands, she closed her spiral notebook. Her favorite pencil with its red, white, and blue Statue of Liberty torch eraser rolled across her desk and fell to the floor. Her dusky face burned as she slowly stood, clutching her backpack. Around her, the class tittered. Frances retrieved the rolling pencil from the floor. Maxzyne reached to take it, but Miss Garrett gave her a withering glance and pointed at the door. Her steely eyes and the arch of her red, thinly penciled brows said she meant business. Maxzyne shuffled out the door knowing somebody would pay for all this classroom drama. *It's my name on the sketch.*

She drags her thoughts back to the present and looks down the deserted hallway. Yikes! The principal's office. Her stomach twists and she burps fish sticks and broccoli from lunch. *Ewwww*. Other than that time she threw up on Alvin Peterson in second grade and the school nurse had to call home, the principal's office is unfamiliar territory.

She trudges forward. Her shoulders sag as her mind races. Maybe she can convince Principal Farwell not to tell her parents. As if. Even if she just gets detention after school, her mother will be waiting to pick her up. She'll know instantly when her daughter doesn't show up out front. Her mother will put this in the category of "very bad behavior unbecoming to a young lady your age." Just thinking about it makes her chew the inside of her lower lip. She gasps. Even worse, tonight is Chicago's Festival of Lights holiday parade! No way she'll get to go if the school principal is involved. Her heart sinks as reality sets in. *Will I be suspended? Just for a stupid drawing?*

Her brain freezes, refusing to imagine the worst. She quickly stuffs the offending sketch into the pocket of her khaki pants. *I'm in way more trouble than pencil smudges on my school uniform. How do I get out of this mess?*

Muffled notes from Miss Garret's autoharp drift into the hallway through the vertical windowpane in the door. The class is singing again. Maxzyne swings her red canvas backpack over her shoulder with resolve. *Time to face the real music.* Principal Farwell.

She strides toward the opposite end of the three-story building. To the right sits her locker, number 316. No point stowing her backpack until she knows what is going to happen. She looks wistfully at the bulletin board announcements posted outside Miss Miranda's Spanish classroom. The tutoring schedule has several names penciled in the blanks. Her eyes slide past the Spanish sign-up sheet. They focus on a poster of tonight's Festival of Lights parade, featuring the school's majorettes.

Sheesh! Maxzyne glares at the smiling troupe of girls in their school colors—gold and navy sequined bodysuits with knee-high white patent leather boots, batons raised in a star-shaped arc. At lunch earlier, Courtney Crowder had the whole table gaga about being in tonight's holiday spectacle. Show-off. Maxzyne fumes, recalling Courtney's reenactment of the tryouts when she and four other girls earned a spot on their Chicago alderman's parade float. Of course, it might have been that ponytail twisting her classmate did when Alderman O'Malley was a guest speaker in their civics class last month. He definitely paid attention when Courtney mentioned her uncle's drugstore chain and parade fund contribution. *She'll be on TV tonight and I'll be grounded till the new year, I bet.* The sudden flash of jealousy makes her burp fish again. Yuck.

She passes the double doors of the cafeteria and wrinkles her nose. There is a whiff of leftover chili, fish sticks, soggy carrots, overcooked broccoli, and steam-cleaned trays. His back to her, Mr. Purcell, the friendly school custodian, pushes a gray mop across the floor. He patiently adds to the already huge pile of dirty napkins, striped straws, and empty milk cartons on the linoleum. Afraid to admit where she's going and why, she walks faster. Grown-ups. Crime and punishment. The principal's office.

On second thought, *I'm already doomed. Why rush?* She slows down, escape plans hatching faster than seagulls on Navy Pier in the spring. Her suede sneakers squeak along the polished floor in the hallway, each step making her consider the impossible. *Hmm . . . What if I don't go to Principal Farwell's office?* Her eyes dart to the wall. A shiny red fire alarm next to the matching fire extinguisher beckons. Last year, one of the sixth-grade boys broke the glass and pulled the alarm just to get out of taking a test. *Nope. Don't even think it.* By the time the police and fire trucks left, he was in a lot more trouble than an "F" on his math exam, she recalls. Definitely suspended. Probably kicked out of school.

"Who gets kicked out of school for doodling in music class?" she groans. Worried, she stops to nibble the end of a slender braid. When she realizes it, she tosses the braid away, disgusted. She stopped chewing her braids in kindergarten! Why couldn't she have been caught doing her math homework instead of drawing Miss Garrett? Then she wouldn't need an excuse *or* an escape plan!

Maxzyne walks on. To her right is the side entrance containing the school's handicapped ramp and oversized doors. In less than two hours, this corridor will be filled with the sound of slamming lockers, and buses will be lined up at the curb outside. Everyone will be excited about the parade later on Michigan Avenue in downtown Chicago. Where will she be? Lockdown.

Better enjoy this last minute of freedom then. Maxzyne leans on the metal and glass exit door, careful not to push it open. Her breath clouds the rectangular glass windowpane as she stares out at the bleak windswept street. *Wait! What's this?* She rubs the misty cloud she made on the cold glass, not quite believing her eyes. *Is that one of the carriage horses galloping straight for the school sidewalk?* She frowns, puzzled. What could be wrong?

A shiny white carriage with plush burgundy seats swings wildly behind the galloping black horse. Strangely, there is nobody in the carriage or guiding the horse. As if to confirm her thoughts, the horse suddenly veers right. Too late, the bouncing carriage clatters over the sidewalk curb. The huge, sweating animal rises on two powerful back legs and is forced to stop.

Maxzyne stares at the rear carriage wheel on the right side nearest to her window. The frantic horse has wedged the tall, old-fashioned wheel into the metal slot of an empty bike rack. Through the thick window glass, she hears the trapped horse whinny in frustration. He is determined to keep moving. She watches the horse ply the air with both front legs, heaving forward. Unable to break loose, the majestic animal tosses his head and his front hooves slam back to the ground. With each desperate lunge, she worries he might get hurt.

In a flash, Maxzyne pushes through the exit door, her red backpack swinging on one shoulder as she runs to the horse. The cold winter air shocks her, despite the long-sleeve navy polo shirt embroidered with the school's gold crest she's wearing. *No time for goose bumps. I've got to help this horse!*

2

Caesar

"WHOA!" SHE SHOUTS, running toward the frightened animal. The horse turns in her direction, trying to see past the dark blinders near his eyes. She skids on the icy sidewalk, barely catching her balance with a one-legged yoga move. "Whoa! Where's your driver?" Her backpack bangs on her hip, and she quickly loops the second strap over her shoulder to secure it.

The horse stops mid-lunge, his flattened ears rising. His muscular chest heaves. He snorts and peers at her curiously. She takes a chance and steps near enough to peek over the edge of the pearly carriage trapped by the wheel. It is empty except for a nubby gray blanket and black silk top hat tossed on the floor. *Weird, huh?* She moves toward the front and traces a brass plaque with cold fingers. It reads "Caesar" in a swirling script. About to burst with curiosity, she steps near the horse's flank and leans closer so he can see her. "Caesar, what's wrong? Where's your driver? Why are you in such a rush?"

The horse pricks his ears in her direction. One large brown eye rolls, half hidden behind the smooth leather blinder. He turns his great head to take a good look at her. His long nose quivers, flecked with foam, and his sweaty flanks heave. He bobs his head, snorting clouds of steam in the cold air.

"Good boy," she croons, daring to touch his soft black cheek. The horse whinnies, tossing his mane as he paws the ground with one hoof. He tries to lunge again, but it is a half-hearted heave forward. The wheel stays firmly trapped in the bike rack.

"Okay, okay. I get it." She steps backward, giving him space. "I bet you want me to fix that carriage wheel, don't you?"

Careful to keep some distance between her and the horse's powerful legs, Maxzyne runs to the trapped carriage wheel. "Okay, Caesar," she calls out. "Just relax! Maybe I can roll it out." The horse cocks his head, seeming to consider her request. Finally, he gives a great sigh. Billowing clouds of moisture rise from his snout. He ducks his head again and impatiently paws the sidewalk with one worn hoof. Then he lunges forward again.

Maxzyne leans hard against the high rear wheel. Wedged tight, it doesn't budge. "Hey! Chillax! I need some slack here!" The horse jerks his head back and whinnies in frustration. *If only I could make him understand me,* she frets. Despite her request, the desperate horse lunges forward again. The high-pitched squeal of scraping metal hurts her ears. She turns to see that the trapped wheel is now twisted at an awkward angle within a slot of the bike rack.

An icy mist is released from a low cloud as it rolls overhead. Maxzyne shivers as a gust of wind whips her dark layers of braids into a crazy halo around her head. She raises a slim brown hand, pulling the woven strands away from her face. Too late, one plastic barrette from a flyaway braid smacks her left cheek.

"Owwww!" she shrieks. With her free hand, she shields her eyes from the gust and the whipping strand with its deadly barrette. The wind rises and she looks skyward. A strange thrumming noise comes from the direction of the school's main entrance. She squints at the American flag as it snaps in the northern breeze. The ropes strain and thrash against the tall pole where it stands guard near the main entrance. Distracted, she almost misses the sudden movement inside the mysterious coach. She blinks three times just to be sure the mist and cold air are not making her imagine things. *Is that really the cool top hat I saw on the carriage floor?*

She watches the elegant accessory sail high on the chilly breeze. Maxzyne is spellbound when it sweeps near her, just out of reach. For several seconds, the lustrous fabric glimmers as it hovers, almost teasing her. Flyaway braids swing loose around her face as she lunges to grab the tempting object. Too late, the hat is swept just out of reach by the invisible fingers of gusting air.

There's something weird going on here. Her eyelashes flutter in surprise to see her face reflected in the glossy black silk as the hat spins several times in front of her. Then, as quickly as it arrived, the wind fades. There is an eerie silence as the wandering hat drifts toward the horse. With a graceful flourish, it drops to the asphalt, landing just behind Caesar's front hooves.

"Whoa, Caesar! What's up with that hat?" she croaks, her breath frosting in the cold air. The horse turns and looks at her. Maxzyne feels the hair on her scalp rise as a flash of electricity races down the back of her neck. Somehow she understands that she is meant to retrieve the curious object. She steps forward and kneels to grab the hat by its brim. As she scoops it up, she has the curious feeling of being watched. A quick glance in Caesar's direction confirms it. His dark head is cocked to the right, with one soft brown eye trained on her. As she stands, he lifts his head, his eye following her. With a nod of approval, he snorts when she pushes the hat securely down over her braids.

Hey, check me out, she brags silently. *I'm going places in this awesome hat!* She preens and adjusts her braids under the brim. Now if only she had a mirror. She tilts the high hat just over her right ear. A gray-speckled feather is tucked in the charcoal hatband where the brim meets the crown, giving it a jaunty dash of style. It's a little too big, even with all her braids, but it's still easy to imagine herself as the carriage mistress. What fun must it be to give people a tour of the city every day? Wearing this hat, she feels positively grand. Her imagination churns. That's her, pointing out the Hancock Building, Millennium Park, and all her favorite cupcake and candy shops. Tourists wouldn't even have to pay her real money—just feed her double Dutch cocoa cupcakes!

"Caesar, do you like cupcakes?" she asks, not really expecting a response to such a silly question. The horse gives a high-pitched whinny and slides his head from side to side, ending with a brief shake of his withers. Maxzyne nearly laughs out loud. This crazy horse just shook his head and practically shrugged his shoulders at the absurdity of her cupcake question.

Caesar whinnies his impatience, shifting restlessly. She straightens her shoulders, suddenly paying attention. "Did you say something?" she asks the horse but then feels silly. *Of course not. Duh! Horses can't talk.* Her mouth drops open in surprise when the horse suddenly bobs his head once. "Huh? Was that a yes?" she squeaks. Caesar drops his head again, this time giving a snort for emphasis. Maxzyne is so startled that she steps backward, pushing the brim of the silk hat out of her eyes. *Is this horse talking for real?*

She stares at him for several seconds before throwing her hands up in the air. "Well, there's one thing we both understand. You need help getting that wheel loose, right?" The horse rumbles a low neigh in response. His great head nods in agreement, and he impatiently taps his right hoof on the asphalt.

"I hear what you're saying. Loud and clear." She shrugs and rolls her eyes. Somehow she accepts that she and the horse seem able to communicate. "And what you're really saying is 'Just do it, already,'" she mutters under her breath. Caesar taps his hoof again and Maxzyne nearly laughs out loud. "Geez. Next you'll be reading my mind! Give me a sec, huh? I'm just getting the hang of things, y'know." Caesar gives a loud sigh, again nodding his head. She starts to remove the hat from her head but suddenly stops. "This hat must be a secret decoder or something. I better hang on to it." The horse neighs in agreement. She tucks a stray braid behind her ear and tilts the hat brim higher on her forehead. Now she can see better. It wobbles a bit, but if she keeps her braids tucked inside, it keeps the hat from falling off.

"C'mon, then! I need your help this time." She strides back to the wheel trapped in the bike rack, one knee on the sidewalk. After a quick blow on her hands to warm them, she pushes with all her strength. With a final, very unladylike grunt that streams from her open mouth, she slowly straightens the twisted wheel on its axle. She rubs her cold fingers together and then flashes a victory sign at the horse. He bobs his head, as if congratulating her. She gives him a half smile and feels a warm flush of pride until the horse neighs impatiently. "Hold your horses," she answers with a giggle. She stands, hands dusting off the knees of her khaki pants. Seconds later, she points at the horse. "Caesar, it's up to you now. Back up and give me some slack." With both hands, she motions for him to move backward and is both surprised and thrilled when the horse takes one step back.

"Yeah, that's it!" she encourages, feeling a bit like Dr. Doolittle talking to animals. "Now come this way. Come on. You got it. Just a smidge more," she wheedles. Amazingly, the horse takes another step backward. She claps and gives him a huge smile. Then, with both hands on the tall, spindly wheel, she pushes hard. The metal is cold, and she grunts louder than ever, trying to move it. The top hat tumbles down over her eyes as she lurches forward, thrilled when the trapped wheel slides out. She gives the silk hat an impatient shove back on her forehead, breathing hard. Working together, she and the horse have somehow managed to free the wheel from the bike rack.

For a moment, even the horse looks surprised. Maxzyne jumps to her feet, pleased by their success. "Way to go! We did it, Caesar! See that? You're free now." She stops jumping and blows on her frozen hands again. This time, the horse just looks at her.

"Well, go on! What're you waiting for? You can go home now! You're free, see? Find your driver. He must be worried." She shivers and claps her hands at the horse. He just rolls his regal head her way, one brown eye blinking and peering at her from beneath the blinder.

"What? You're not talking now? What's up with that?" She frowns, stepping closer. "Hey! You're not lost, are you?" Maxzyne reaches high, daring to stroke his proud neck. This time he allows her fingers to trail across his windswept mane. "Don't you want to get home?" she croons. "There must be a nice warm barn with lots of hay to eat somewhere, right?"

His ears prick at her again. "That's a word you understand, isn't it? H-A-Y." The horse nods his head and whinnies loudly. Maxzyne continues stroking his tangled mane, thinking out loud. "So if someone's looking for you and . . ." She pauses, thinking hard as she winds a braid back under the brim of her hat. "Wait a minute . . . I found *you*, didn't I?" The horse nods again, the leather bridle with its silver trim tinkling. Maxzyne rocks back and forth on her flat suede sneakers, a huge smile crossing her face. "Sure did! So I'll just find your owner. Won't he be glad I got you unstuck? Grateful, even!" Her eyes slide past the carriage and down the deserted street. "I mean, I could really use some extra credit with the grown-ups right now."

She glances back at the blank windows of the school cafeteria. Maybe it's just luck, but it seems no one has seen her outside yet. Relieved, she takes a deep breath. "Okay, Caesar. Maybe you and I can help each other, huh?" The ebony horse throws back his head as if in agreement. The mane on his proud neck ripples in a sudden gust of wind.

Caught off guard, Maxzyne jumps backward to the sidewalk. "Hey, buddy. Warn me if you're gonna make a move like that!" She throws her arms up, and the horse neighs. With a shrug, she clamps the hat down tighter on her head. "Just saying." Her teeth chatter with cold, and her lips feel like sandpaper. She bounces on her toes and rubs her arms for warmth. That's when she remembers the gray blanket.

The graceful white carriage with its plush, tufted seat and shiny brass light sconces are just a step away. The next damp gust of wind convinces her to climb up. Seconds later, she is grateful to be wrapped in the blanket's musty cocoon. She hugs the rough wool tightly around her body and sits down on the high driver's seat. Once the heat slowly returns to her hands and face, it isn't long until her gaze is drawn back to the school building.

What now? Dry leaves rustle and scrape against the sidewalk curb in the chilly breeze. She huddles under the blanket, trying to decide. As if making up her mind for her, Caesar gives a loud snort and leans forward, pulling the carriage down the street. Twenty yards behind the carriage, a car turns the corner at the intersection and glides past. Maxzyne emerges from the blanket and waves, at the last second remembering to raise the brim of the old-fashioned hat. She gives it a jaunty sweep, just like she's seen the carriage drivers do on Michigan Avenue. The car driver sees her and responds with two quick honks. She is thrilled, but the noise spooks Caesar. With a fierce whinny, the horse lunges forward and strains against the harness. There is a crash of hooves on asphalt as the horse breaks into a desperate gallop. Up ahead and already half a block away, the car turns a corner and disappears from view.

Surprised by Caesar's reaction, Maxzyne is thrown back against the driver's seat, the silk hat toppling into the back seat. She ditches the blanket and scrambles into the safety of the rear passenger seat.

"Whoa! Caesar! Whoa!" she screeches. The carriage lurches from the sidewalk and into the street. Ignoring her shrieks, the horse picks up the pace. Worse, it's as if her screams only make the animal move faster. *So much for Dr. Doolittle.*

The top hat bounces to the carriage floor. Terrified, Maxzyne quickly follows. With a gasp, she drops to her knees. Unable to keep her balance, she finally sits on the floor, holding on for dear life. The coach clatters down the deserted street, thrown off balance by the slightly bent rear wheel. As it hurtles away from the familiar school grounds, she hears a faint metallic ringing over the thunder of Caesar's pounding hooves. *Yikes! Could it be . . . ?* She stays seated on the carriage floor, afraid to turn around and look back. There is no mistaking the shrill clanging of her middle school's bell. *Fifth period. If I live through this, I am so doomed.*

3

Rico and Rosa

AS THE HORSE CHARGES AHEAD, Maxzyne screams, "Whoa, Caesar! Stop! Hey!" She rises to her knees, her brown knuckles pale from the effort of holding on. "Did you hear me? I said you can stop now!" Her command turns into a whimper. "P-p-please?"

Her voice slides up an octave and ends in a wobbly screech. Desperate, she grabs the blanket from the driver's perch in front and throws it forward. The fuzzy edge brushes the horse's flank. Unfortunately, the gray wool catches the wind and whips right back into her face. Instead of slowing the horse, she has just scared him into a full gallop. "Whoa, boy, whoa! Somebody get me out of here!" she yelps. Terrified, she collapses in a heap under the prickly weight of the blanket.

"If only I'd gone straight to the principal's office like I was supposed to," she wails. "Anything's better than being dead on arrival!" Finding it hard to breathe through the thick wool, she struggles to rise to her knees again. With her left elbow around the coach's dash rail for balance, she uses her other hand to escape the blanket. After the musty wool, the brisk air feels good. She gulps the fine icy mix as her grateful lungs expand. *Breathe. Stay calm and breathe.*

Suddenly, the horse veers right. The coach lurches, defying gravity as it rises dangerously on two right wheels. Maxzyne can hear the scrape of one damaged wheel on the asphalt. With a bloodcurdling yelp, she slides to the right, banging her elbow.

"I guess you only understand me when I wear the hat!" she screams at the horse. She stretches one arm toward the black hat and quickly grabs it by the brim. The horse pays no attention. Instead, he continues his frantic gallop down the deserted street. It takes only a second to jam the hat back over her braids. She holds on to the hat with one hand and screeches, "Stop! Can you hear me? I said, 'Stop!'"

At last, Caesar slows down. His hooves crunch and the carriage wheels roll on what now sounds like dirt and gravel. The horse brays and slows to a walk. She dares to peer over the rail just as someone shouts, "Whoa, *amigo* (friend)!"

Caesar whinnies louder as Maxzyne tries to stand. She hangs on to the cold brass rail and stares as a lanky boy about her age runs toward the horse. His topaz-flecked eyes flash with determination as he fearlessly leaps into Caesar's path. Maxzyne watches, her heart catching in her throat. There is a slow-motion battle between boy and beast for what seems like a long minute. The horse plunges forward, but the strange boy refuses to back down. At the last second, he reaches in to grab the loose leather reins. She marvels at how he expertly sidesteps Caesar's powerful hooves. The stranger then leans away from the horse, pulling the reins taut.

"*¡Hola! ¿Qué pasa?*" (Hey! What's up?) he asks the horse. The boy is careful to hold on to the reins tightly. Using both feet to brake, he drags his scuffed leather boots through the dirt and gravel. His dark eyes sparkle as he takes control of the wild horse.

"Why the hurry, mi amigo?" He makes an odd clicking noise with his tongue, and the horse lowers his head, snorts, and finally stops. Maxzyne hangs over the brass rail, grateful the carriage is at last still. They both watch Caesar, steam clouds rising from his nostrils and around his head. The boy gives Maxzyne a triumphant grin. She barely has time to notice his gleaming teeth and high, tanned cheekbones as a sudden gust of wind tosses his jet-black hair across his face. With an impatient hand, he sweeps the wavy locks away and stares at her.

"His name's Caesar," she offers. "Says right there, see?" Maxzyne points to the brass plaque on the white surrey. "Thanks for putting the brakes on him. Good thing, 'cause I thought we wouldn't stop till Canada!"

The boy nods and shrugs. "*De nada.*" (It's nothing.)

A shy silence grows between them as they gaze at the horse. Caesar's head hangs low and his great chest heaves, with each breath growing slower. Frosty air swirls from his velveteen nostrils. The boy wraps the reins tight around his hand and leans near the horse. Maxzyne hears him murmur softly, "*Está bien.* (That's good.) Take your time, amigo. You are safe here."

Curious about the boy, her eyes dart around the courtyard. *What is this place?* The gravel path leads to several brick-and-stone outbuildings with huge arched openings. The architecture looks solid and old-fashioned. Nothing like the skyscrapers she is used to seeing in her city Loop neighborhood. Bales of straw are piled to one side, and there are droppings of manure scattered throughout the well-trod dirt portion of the path. She is startled when the boy calmly walks Caesar across the adjoining yard to a long metal trough near the central arch. The horse whinnies in appreciation. "That's definitely 'thanks' in horse talk," Maxzyne offers. Caesar lowers his head and slurps water with his long, dark tongue.

Without warning, the stranger whirls around. He shakes his fist at her and his eyes flash. "Why treat a horse this way?" he asks in halting English. "*Está asustado.* (He's scared.) And so thirsty." He jerks his thumb at the water trough before pointing to a jagged scar on the horse's right flank. She watches as he examines it carefully. Finally, he bends down on one knee to take a closer look at Caesar's worn gray hooves. Above him, the horse shifts nervously. With a deep frown, the boy rises, hands on his hips. "You do this to him for the money?" He glares at her.

His anger catches her by surprise. "Huh? What do you mean?" she blusters. "I tried to help! It's not my fault he went crazy. Something scared him." To make her point, she leaps from the carriage, but her dark tangle of braids bounce free when the tall silk hat falls backward, landing on the floor of the carriage. It is quickly forgotten as Maxzyne's nose curls in dismay. *Ewwww.* She has landed inches away from a pile of fresh horse droppings on the ground. She teeters dangerously on one foot before doing a short bunny hop away from the mess. Grateful to be back on clean, solid ground, she stands tall and straight, ignoring the strange boy's stare.

He steps toward the thirsty horse, his voice rising to accuse her again. "*¡Sí!* (Yes!) He is scared! For his life! *Carros, autobuses, motocicletas, ambulancias.* (Cars, buses, motorcycles, ambulances.) For a horse in the city—*es malo* (it's bad). Noise. Smoke in his face all day." He strokes Caesar and shakes his head. A deep frown wrinkles his forehead and hardens his eyes. "This horse has lost his soul. It was stolen from him and for what?" The angry boy points to the scar on Caesar's flank and glares at her.

"*Dinero,*" (Money) he hisses.

Maxzyne's face burns as she sputters. "But everyone loves carriage rides! Especially on Michigan Avenue. The tourists always take pictures. Besides, my dad says it's good for business when—"

"Bah! *¡Turistas!* (Tourists!) Business!"

Maxzyne is shocked when the boy steps close and pokes her in the arm.

"You make this horse a slave for turistas?" His voice cracks like a whip. "Steal his soul for business?" He slices one hand through the air as if ending the idea and their conversation once and for all. His eyes narrow as he points a finger at her. "You do not deserve this horse!"

"You think I—wait! Me? Own a horse? Now *you're* the crazy one!"

"You calling me *loco* (crazy)?" he sneers. "The only crazy is you with this horse! A horse that breaks his back all day on city streets. And what is his reward?" The boy's eyes flash amber sparks again.

Maxzyne is mad enough to kick horse poop at this rude kid accusing her of horse abuse, but that would ruin her shoes. Instead, she straightens her shoulders and sticks her chin out, hands on her hips. "No way! Not me! For such a know-it-all, you don't know anything, do you?" she sneers, but her voice wobbles just a bit. *Why does this always happen around boys? Just when you need to prove a point?* She fumes. *Breathe.* She fills her lungs, the icy air giving her confidence. "Hey! News flash," she continues. "He's *not my horse*! Get it?"

The boy shakes his head and points at her head. "You forget the hat! I saw it! You are the driver." He stares her down. To her credit, she blinks several times before looking away. *No way I tell* him *about the magic hat. He thinks he knows so much about horses. Well, I can talk to them!*

"So?" the boy interrupts her private thoughts. "What do you say, News Flash, Know-it-all?"

Her eyes slide toward the carriage as she ignores his smug jeer. *Ha! I'll show him!* Before he can stop her, she climbs halfway up into the carriage. The black top hat is trapped between the seat bench and her red canvas backpack. She leans forward and reaches for the backpack, easily slinging the strap over her shoulder. Then she grabs the hat and jumps back down to the ground. With an exaggerated sweep of the hat to the top of her head, she gives a defiant smirk. The hat drops over her braids. She lets the hat sink low on her forehead, not bothering to tuck away her braids. She squints at him from beneath the brim.

"See? It doesn't fit 'cause it's *not* mine. I was just, er, trying it out. Before that, I was only trying to help a runaway horse. Nobody was even in the carriage. So there!" She resists the urge to stick out her tongue at him.

The slim stranger frowns and points. "Then you helped yourself to someone else's horse!" he crows.

"Whaaat? You mean, like, stole him?" She gasps. "Why would I steal a horse? We live in a condo!"

For once, the boy looks uncertain. "Condo?"

"Yeah." She points above her head. "You know. High-rise in the sky? Fifty-seven flights of stairs? Now *that* would be animal abuse! They don't even let dogs on the lobby elevators in my building. They have to take the freight elevator instead. And I don't think that's *big* enough for him." She points at the horse, unable to hold back a grin. Just thinking about Caesar riding in her building's freight elevator up to meet her shocked parents makes her giggle. She claps a hand over her mouth, nearly giving herself the hiccups.

The boy suddenly smiles back, revealing two perfect dimples in his cheeks. *He's kinda cute when he smiles.* She is immediately annoyed with herself for thinking such a silly thing and fights the urge to blush. The two of them look at Caesar. Glancing from the horse to each other, they both start to laugh.

"Floor twenty-one, please," Maxzyne requests as she steps forward. This time, she is careful not to step in a manure pile. She pretends to push an elevator button. "After you, please." She sweeps her arm toward the horse.

The strange boy laughs louder. He drops the reins, but Caesar suddenly rears up, his front legs pawing the air above him.

"Look out!" Maxzyne shrieks. She jumps backward as the horse slams his front hooves back to the ground. He shakes his head and bares his teeth before giving a loud whinny. "Geez, we were just kidding, Caesar! Nobody meant to make fun of you." She clutches the hat to her head as her stomach lurches half-digested fish sticks. "Hey, any chance he might be hungry?"

"Whoa! Whoa!" Again, the boy makes several soothing chirps and quickly grabs the reins. He pulls the leather straps taught and pats the horse on the flank. "Good boy. We go inside. Maybe she does know something about horses, eh? You want to eat, amigo?" With a flick of the reins and more strange clicks of his tongue, the young horseman leads Caesar toward one of the stone archways.

"You coming, High-rise?" The boy turns to her and waits. An impish grin again makes two perfect dimples in his tan cheeks. Maxzyne gives a nonchalant shrug before whipping the hat from her head and striding after them. She keeps a close eye on Caesar's hooves as she walks, unzipping her backpack and stuffing the hat inside.

"So I'm right, huh? He's hungry," she confirms, trying not to sound too smug.

The boy's long fingers brush Caesar's flank as the trio reaches the nearest stone archway. "Horses are *always* hungry! *Todo el tiempo*." (All the time.) The stranger's laugh catches in his throat. He looks at her as though she just asked the dumbest question in the world.

She tries not to notice. "How come you know so much about horses? What's your name, anyway?" They step into the shadow of the arched entrance. Once inside, Maxzyne is surprised to see a towering stack of hay bales in one corner of the slightly warmer interior. "Is this a barn? In the middle of the city?"

"How come you ask so many questions, High-rise?" He doesn't give her a chance to answer. "Not just a barn. This is the historic Old Horse Theatre of Chicago!" The boy bows low from the waist, arms outstretched, as if welcoming her to a grand palace. "A place that respects horses," he adds, "for being the smartest and noblest animals on earth." Again, he can't quite hide his smirk.

He leads Caesar to a nearby trough filled with golden grain. The horse ducks his head, eager to eat. From the far corner there is a gentle whinny. Maxzyne turns to see several other horses eyeing them through the wooden slats in a long row of closed stall doors. Caesar's ears prick in their direction, but he continues to eat. The horse munches as flecks of grain catch on his whiskers and velvet nose.

Eager to know more, she thrusts out her hand. "My name's Maxzyne, actually. That's with an x, z, and y," she adds.

"X, z, and y?" The boy ignores her hand and looks at her curiously.

"Yeah. Just think of all the Scrabble points you get spelling my name. Prob'ly enough to win the game." Self-conscious again, she lets her hand drop back to her side.

"You always talk so much, High-rise, er, Max—with an x, z, and y?" His eyebrows rise in amusement.

"Only when I'm not sure who I'm talking to," she retorts. "I mean, maybe if you told me *your* name . . . ?" She sticks out her chin and waits.

"*Perdón, me llamo Rico.*" (Pardon, my name is Rico.) His name rolls off his tongue, sounding a bit exotic. With a graceful flourish, he transfers Caesar's reins to his left hand and offers her a calloused right hand. Pleased with his polite gesture, she grins. His firm grip is warm as he briefly clasps her pencil-smudged fingers.

"So what is your plan *con este caballo* (with this horse)?" He jerks his head at Caesar, who contentedly munches beside him. "You will not ride him to your condo, eh?"

She ignores his tease about the condo. Suddenly nervous, her words tumble out in a rush. "Well, I figure if I can find his owner, do something positive, then maybe I wouldn't be in so much trouble. Uh, that is, after getting kicked out of class for drawing Miss Garrett." She pauses, not liking how that sounded. "Well, Miss Garrett's my music teacher, see? And it wasn't really my fault." She flaps her arms dramatically. "I mean, I was bored, so I just started doodling this cartoon and the other kids took it and—hey!" She stomps her foot and her hazel eyes flash. "Why are you laughing?" She frowns and stands tall, resting both hands on her hips.

"You sure got a lot of words in you, High-rise." Rico shakes his head. He doesn't smile, but his eyes twinkle.

Maxzyne bristles. "Well, at least I tried to do something. I mean, I got the horse here, didn't I?" She tosses her braids away from her face, daring him to make fun of her again.

"True." He nods, too polite to remind her that he was the one who actually stopped the runaway horse and carriage. "But who is the owner? Where do we find him?" Beside him, Caesar lifts his head from the feed trough and whinnies. His head rolls from either side of his powerful neck as if he disagreed with these particular questions. From behind one of the stall doors, there is an answering whinny. *Caesar doesn't sound very positive about that plan*, she thinks.

Rico rubs Caesar's long snout. "The owner does not deserve this horse!" The boy scowls and his eyes flash dangerously. "El caballo can't be trusted on the streets when there is so much stress in him." He walks behind Caesar, but this time remembers to make a few reassuring clicks of his tongue.

Is that some sort of horse code? Maxzyne wonders. She watches as he easily unfastens the carriage tethered to the horse's carriage lines.

"Uh . . . we?" Her voice rises. "When did *my* rescue mission become *we*? So far, all you've done is water and feed him."

"So you know caballos and don't any need help?" Rico shrugs at her. He doesn't wait for an answer but tugs the reins. She follows as he leads Caesar to the row of stall doors.

The young horseman jerks his thumb back toward Maxzyne. "What do you think of that, Caesar?" Now curious about the other horses in the stalls, Caesar eagerly follows the boy's lead. Maxzyne must lengthen her stride to keep up.

"Well, um, no . . . prob'ly not enough to . . . I mean, if you want to help, that's great. But . . . well, okay—it's cool. Besides, what if we don't find the owner?" He doesn't answer. She catches up to them and waits as he opens an empty stall door. The boy gently ushers Caesar inside. With a firm hand, he strokes the horse's back. This motion seems to calm Caesar as he snuffles and turns, finally settling comfortably in his new space. Maxzyne continues her train of thought. "Yeah, why not? Maybe we'll just save the horse."

Rico steps outside the stall door. He gives a final reassuring tongue click to Caesar and closes the door. He smiles through the slats. "You are safe here, amigo." He glances into the adjoining stall. "Lady Pearl will keep you company. Sí, *princesa* (princess)?"

His grin widens as he waves several fingers at a platinum mare sporting a thick golden mane. Maxzyne peers through the slats and admires the beautiful horse. *All Lady Pearl needs is a long horn and she'd be a unicorn from the storybooks I used to draw.* As if reading her thoughts, the horse shuffles closer. Lady Pearl blinks, one gray eye with long golden lashes, observing the young girl through the slats.

From the other side of the long row of stalls comes a high-pitched whistle. Rico looks over his shoulder, his face tense, but relaxes when a pretty girl with a smile just like his own strides toward them. Maxzyne stares at her. She secretly admires the other girl's shiny dark hair as it falls over a tan turtleneck and brown leather riding jacket. Her knee-high boots are a soft black and perfectly flat. She carries a riding crop in her slim brown hand.

"*¿Dónde has estado, Rico?*" (Where have you been?) Her voice is smooth and accented. She looks at Maxzyne curiously. "And who is she?"

Maxzyne steps forward. "Hi. My name's Maxzyne." She feels very out of place in her school uniform but extends her hand to the girl.

"With an x, z, and y," Rico adds, again trying not to smile. Maxzyne rolls her eyes in annoyance. *Why do boys always have to make fun of girls every chance they get?*

"This is Rosa, my sister," he shrugs nonchalantly.

The pretty girl accepts Maxzyne's handshake and wrinkles her nose at her brother. "Sí, your older twin sister was sent to find you. You are late for practice."

She drops Maxzyne's hand, turning serious. "Now Mr. Stryker is *enojado* (upset). What are you doing out here? What is she doing here?" Rosa glances at the school crest on Maxzyne's polo shirt. She points to the light suede school shoes. "Those shoes won't be clean for long. Not in here!"

"Forget her shoes. Help me with *este carro* (this carriage)." Rico races down the dim row of stalls. He motions to the two girls. "Quick. We must hide it!"

They race after him and skid to a stop just as Rico pulls a long gray tarp from a hook high on a worn wooden post. The canvas cloth falls to the ground, raising a cloud of fine golden straw bits around them.

"Ah-choo!" Maxzyne sneezes when the dust cloud reaches her nose.

Rico ignores her sneeze. "*¡Rápido!*" (Hurry!) He drags the tarp to the white carriage abandoned earlier near the feed trough.

"Where did you get this carriage?" Rosa demands. She frowns when he doesn't answer. He unfurls the tarp and each girl grabs a corner of the canvas, lifting it. Rico jumps inside the carriage and reaches for it.

"You'll get us in trouble, Rico," his twin scolds. "Mr. Stryker won't like it. You know we can't lose this job."

"Who's Mr. Stryker?" Puzzled, Maxzyne looks from one twin to the other. "Do you *work* here?"

"Not for long," Rosa snaps. She jerks her edge of the canvas tarp and straightens it over the carriage. "He'll get us fired!" She glares at her brother. "For being late to practice and bringing something that does not belong here: trouble!" She stands with both hands on her hips, daring him to respond.

Rico doesn't look at her. Instead, he leaps from the far side of the carriage, neatly pulling the tarp down around the carriage wheels. "Get a few bales of hay to put in front here and nobody will see it," he insists.

His twin sister stands firm. Rico gives an exaggerated sigh. "Rosa, *es mi problema* (it's my problem), not yours."

"We are twins, *hermanito* (little brother). What you do hurts me too," she hisses back. "And what about her?" Rosa jerks her thumb at Maxzyne.

He shrugs. "She found the horse. Now he is safe."

Rosa is dismayed. "Horse!" she screeches.

"Just help her hide under the carriage while we practice." He gives Maxzyne a strained smile "Okay, High-rise?"

"*¡Un momento!* (One minute!) Horse? What horse, Rico?" Rosa slaps the canvas cloth with her riding crop.

Rico shakes his head. "Later, *hermanita* (little sister)." He pulls up an edge of the tarp and impatiently points under the carriage, waiting for Maxzyne. She frowns and backs away, one hand clutching her backpack.

"Uh, let me get this straight. You want me to wait here while you go practice . . . what, exactly?"

Her shoulders sag when he nods. "¡Sí, rápido!"

She rolls her eyes, slowly crawls past the hay bales, and ducks under the tarp. "Don't know why I can't just go with you and—"

"Stay there," he orders. "I'll come get you." As an afterthought, he pushes the gray blanket under the carriage.

Maxzyne sits cross-legged on the cold stone floor. The twins' feet recede from view as they walk away. She watches Rosa kick a small pile of straw at her brother.

"Are you crazy?" Rosa hisses. "You brought a strange horse and this girl to the Old Horse Theatre? *¡Cielos!* (Heavens!) Our family will lose this job, Rico. Our paychecks. Everything!"

Both twins' boots disappear and their voices grow faint. "*¡Relájate!*" (Relax!) Rico urges. "Of course, I will take care of it. I promise. Come on—we are late."

Still bickering, they walk down the long row of stalls toward another set of high arches. Seconds later, from the far end of the building, a door squeaks on ancient metal hinges and closes behind them. Maxzyne sighs, grateful for the rustling, munching, and shuffling sounds of horses in their stalls nearby. In the shadowy gloom of the stable, she anxiously waits for Rico's return.

4

The Old Horse Theatre

SINCE WHEN DID I BECOME SUCH A WIMP? Maxzyne frets as she crouches beneath the carriage in the dark. Why didn't she stand up to Rico when he told her to hide? Her knees begin to ache and her feet tingle. *How long does he expect me to wait here, anyway?* For the second time that day, she wraps herself in the wool carriage blanket.

She tugs a braid toward her mouth, thinking hard. She frowns. *Who would know if she hid and watched them practice, anyway? Practice what, though? Something with horses and his family, and they get paid for it. Wait, how can kids even be working?* The questions multiply. They swirl in her head until she can't bear to hide under the carriage for another second. With one hand on the blanket, she crawls past the damaged carriage wheel and stands. Her knees are sore as she brushes bits of dirt and straw from her khaki pants.

She pulls her backpack from beneath the carriage and decides to check on the silk top hat. *Might as well wear it, right?* She unzips the canvas bag and retrieves the glossy hat before piling her braids and barrettes into a messy bunch and stuffing them under the silk brim. She looks around the deserted stable area. *Nobody's even here to see me,* she fumes. *Just who made Rico the boss, anyway?* "I'm Maxzyne 'the Greatest' Merriweather! And if you don't know me, you don't *know me!*" she declares. Wearing the hat definitely gives her confidence.

She picks up the blanket and decides it might come in handy later. *Uh-oh. Later. I don't want to think about later.* She peers inside the red backpack, choosing what to keep. *Definitely don't need the math textbook or English workbook.* She drops them behind the carriage wheel and kicks straw around them. *Keep the pencils and lined notebook paper, just in case. An artist always needs her tools, right?* Her quick brown hands expertly fold the blanket edges together and she rolls the musty wool into a tight cylinder that fits in the bottom of her backpack. Seconds later she shrugs her shoulders back into the straps, tightening them securely. Eager to do something other than wait, she tries to justify leaving the hiding place. "Hey, like Dad always says about his work, 'Being too cautious is the greatest risk of all,'" she mutters. Her legs wobble a bit as she walks down the stall corridor on tingling feet. "So I'm gonna see what's going on."

First, she makes a beeline for Caesar's stall. She peeks through the door slats and smiles to see his long nose directly facing Lady Pearl's window slats where they share an adjoining wall. The pale female horse does the same, making it seem as though they are having an intimate conversation. She has the distinct impression that Caesar is telling Lady Pearl how difficult life has been on the city streets. His fat lips vibrate as he makes a low rumbling noise and his tail switches back and forth. The woeful story continues with his sale to a carriage driver. Maxzyne's shoulders slump as she senses his feelings of loss and abandonment. Through the adjoining stall window slats, Lady Pearl sighs and snuffles. The pretty horse's gentle nickers seem to console Caesar's sadness. He heaves a great sigh, and for a moment his tail is still. It is such a private conversation that Maxzyne feels guilty eavesdropping on them.

Wait. Did I just hear Caesar talking? Oh yes, I did! Wow, this hat is the real deal. She pushes a stray braid back under the brim, her mind racing. Ever since trying it on, she felt she could understand this animal. And Rico thinks he knows so much about horses! She waits, curious to hear more. Caesar snuffles and moves restlessly around the stall, continuing to tell Lady Pearl about his past. Maxzyne has an impression of the horse performing on a stage, but she loses the image when her backpack bumps the stall door and gives her away. Both horses turn in unison to look at her through the door slats. They stamp their hooves and whinny with annoyance at the interruption.

Embarrassed at being caught listening, she waves at them. "Hey there! Uh, sorry to interrupt. Don't worry 'bout me . . . I'm just going to go watch Rico and Rosa practice. Glad to see you're getting to know each other. Talk later, huh? Bye!" She steps away, feeling self-conscious as their solemn eyes follow her down the hall.

Moving toward the big arched doors, she spots a black jacket similar to Rosa's. It hangs high on a hook near some rakes, shovels, and other riding gear. How to reach it? She spies an empty metal pail and quickly flips it over. Pleased with her ingenuity, she uses it as a step stool. Fortunately, it is just high enough, and she pulls the jacket from its hook. The shoulders feel snug, but it seems to fit once it is buttoned over her navy polo shirt. Although the leather sleeves hang down to her knuckles, she rolls them into cuffs and considers it a fashion success. At least she feels warmer. She also decides to return the hat to her backpack for safekeeping. Besides, she can move faster without it.

Now where did Rico and Rosa go? She continues past the long line of closed stall doors toward the arched doors at the far end of the long, dusty corridor. Overhead, bare bulbs on the ancient ceiling are thick with abandoned spider webs. Their weak beams of light only exaggerate the shadows. The stable area smells of hay, horse manure, and oiled leather. There is something reassuring about such natural scents and the sound of contented horses in their stalls.

A soft whinny distracts her. She pauses to peek through the slats of the nearest closed stall door. A sturdy chestnut horse, with a coffee-colored mane and milk-tinged ears, playfully nudges his velvet nose against the slat. She clicks her tongue on the roof of her mouth. It's a reasonable attempt to sound like Rico, but doesn't work. She gives the horse a lopsided grin and shrugs. "Sorry, amigo." The horse snuffles, one skeptical eye on her hands. She waves to prove they are empty. "I wish I had an apple or carrot to give you, but I'm fresh out. I'll check with Rico when I see him, though." She reaches through the slat and strokes the perfect diamond star under his dark mane and then turns away.

At the far end of the horse paddock, the huge double door suddenly cracks open with a creaking wail. The stable floor is splashed with strange rays of blue, red, and golden light. Maxzyne shrinks back against the stall door.

"I'll get *El Capitán* (The Captain) while you go over it again with Rosa," a gruff male voice announces. Quickly, Maxzyne unhooks the stall door latch behind her. This disturbs the young chestnut horse that shifts restlessly.

"Shhhhhh," she whispers, closing the door behind her. She puts her finger to her lips and ducks below the slatted door window. The horse shuffles around her. Curious, he sniffs her neck and nudges her backpack loose, hoping to find a treat. Oh, how it tickles! She tries not to giggle, but his warm breath and soft nose on her neck are hard to ignore. She clutches the backpack to her chest as she hides and listens.

In the corridor, heavy footsteps stop at a nearby stall. She hears the latch slide and the door swing open as the growly voice demands, "Time's up, El Capitán. Gotta work for all that special feed you've been chowing down. If we get a good crowd for tonight's show, maybe I won't have a heart attack when I see this month's feed bill." The horse responds with a throaty neigh. There is a shuffle of hooves as riding gear is quickly cinched. She hears the sound of a palm smacking the horse's flank. In a rush of man and beast, they exit the stall and head back to the mysterious doors at the end of the hall. The rusty hinges groan again as the huge doors close. She breathes a sigh of relief. *Whew! Close call.*

She slowly stands and peers through the door slat. "The coast is clear," she whispers to the curious horse beside her. She unzips her backpack to check its contents. After hugging it so tightly, the top hat is somewhat wrinkled around the brim. She carefully smoothes the fabric with her fingers and blows on the feather tucked into the hatband. Satisfied, she twirls it once on her fingers then returns it to the backpack and zips the canvas closed. Slipping the straps over her shoulders again, she turns back to the chestnut horse and waves. "Back to my mission," she whispers. "Later!" She opens the door and darts into the corridor. The eager horse tries to follow her, but the stall door quickly closes. With a neigh of disappointment, he shuffles back to his trough filled with hay.

Outside the stall, Maxzyne is careful to stay near the shadowy edges of the dusty corridor. With a watchful eye on the huge doors ahead, she jogs toward them.

Breathe. Her lungs fill, but her heart races. *What's going on in there?* she wonders. On her tiptoes, she reaches for one of the high iron handles on the heavy wood doors. The curved metal is rough and cool to the touch. She pulls the right door open just a crack, wincing as the old hinges squeal. Afraid of discovery, she waits several seconds before peering into the adjoining space.

What's this? She blinks several times as her eyes adjust to the glare of flashing red and gold lights. Adding to the confusion, a blast of music becomes a burst of chatter as a loudspeaker whines and crackles. A familiar male voice demands attention. It is the raspy, commanding voice of the man she'd heard in El Capitán's stall moments before. *That must be the boss,* she guesses. Growing bolder, she cracks the door open a few inches wider, curiosity overcoming her fear of discovery.

"Give Rosa more time to stand, Rico! Think drama! Get folks out of their seats 'cause they think she might fall. C'mon, faster! Tease some more applause out of 'em, Rosa! It's your moment, so grab 'em by the hearts and squeeze."

Maxzyne spots a burly man with a microphone at the far end of an indoor performance ring surrounded by wood bleachers. He waves his plaid flannel baseball cap at the two familiar figures galloping past on horseback. Their horse, El Capitán, stirs up small tornadoes of dust under his speeding hooves. Her own heart squeezes tightly when Rico suddenly pulls up the reins. Horse and riders brake to a dramatic stop at the far end of the arena.

"Not bad, but not quite good enough," the man growls. "You kids take another lap. Rosa, turn around on the back of the horse and do that 'look, no hands' move again." The twins glance at each other and then resettle themselves on the saddle. Rico stands in the stirrups. Rosa sits in the saddle behind him, neck and shoulders straight, head held high. "Go on, one more time," the man urges. He points the microphone at them. "Oh, yeah. And don't forget: halfway back, switch to one foot. That's always a showstopper."

Rico hugs the horse with his heels. He lightly taps the riding crop on the animal's shining flanks, and the handsome twins and horse repeat their quick trot around the ring.

"Faster, Rico!" the man barks over the loudspeaker. "Let her hook one foot behind you. Yeah, that's it. Good, good. Now give her the fan to hold."

Amazed by their skill, Maxzyne's mouth drops open. Rosa stands upright, balancing on horseback with outstretched arms. El Capitán's hooves match the fast tempo of the music as Rico retrieves a golden fan from inside his leather jacket. The swirling colored spotlights make its rhinestone trim sparkle. With a dramatic sweep of his arm, he offers it to her. Rosa smiles broadly and flips it open. Her shiny black hair streams behind her as she waves the gilt fan high above her head before daring to stand backward on the speeding horse's back.

"That's it!" Excited, the husky man punches the air with his fist. "Now, smile like you mean it, Lady Rose!" The young horsewoman flashes a dazzling smile as she turns gracefully in the saddle again. "Keep turning and you'll knock 'em dead. That's one heck of a heart-attack move on horseback!" He points behind the ring railing. "Everyone else be ready to partner up for the Spanish dance grand finale once they're done."

There is a smattering of applause and piercing whistles. Maxzyne glimpses a small crowd of waiting riders watching from the arena sidelines. Many are sitting on horses of their own.

She decides it's best to stay out of sight. If she stays near the stable door of the Old Horse Theatre, she should be safe. It's hard to hide, though, when she can barely take her eyes off Rosa. The graceful young performer is standing tall on a huge *trotting* horse. Somehow able to defy physics and gravity, Rosa raises one leg behind her, arms outstretched and back arched. Amazingly, just one foot is balancing her on the horse. The golden fan flashes above her head.

Wow. And I thought yoga was hard, standing on a mat with both feet on the floor. Maxzyne's heart skips a beat. She's amazed by the girl's poise and balance, despite the danger. Content to let his sister shine, Rico urges the horse on with delicate flicks of the riding crop. Adding to the excitement, tiny floodlights blink and twinkle in time to the music. The scene turns magical when hidden spouts under the ring release a fine mist that rises around the performers. Clouds of shimmering lavender and gold slowly rise around the horse as the rehearsal continues. Without an audience in the bleachers, the classical music echoes in the empty arena. Maxzyne holds fast to the railing each time the ground trembles, fearing the worst as the galloping horse and riders pass her hiding place.

So Rico really does know horses, she marvels. *And Rosa is awesome!* She tries to imagine how it must feel to be them, two fearless performers practicing their complicated routine. As if reading her mind, Rico raises his hand and expertly flips his sister into the saddle. Rosa sits behind him and waves to imaginary spectators in the empty arena. The music slows, colorful lights fade to white, and the mist slowly clears.

Now Rico gives a new command. The majestic horse stops in the center of the ring and bows low to the ground on his knees. The twins hold hands and raise them together before gracefully leaping from the saddle to stand beside him. There is a hushed silence as the arena lights dim to black.

Maxzyne blinks, straining to see through the inky darkness. She waits, grateful when a solitary spotlight illuminates the horse and its young riders. They flash dazzling smiles at the empty seats and bow in unison. Rising together, they turn to clap for the proud kneeling horse. The spotlight fades as the harsh overhead lights of the arena brighten the ring.

"That's good, kids. Real nice," the gruff voice purrs through the loudspeaker. "Play it like that tonight. Create some buzz on opening night, and this show's gonna be standing room only all season!"

The loudspeaker crackles and thumps when the microphone is accidentally dropped. There is a painful screech followed by the sound of shuffling papers. From the far side of the ring, the man in charge waves a handful of glossy flyers. Maxzyne watches him motion

Rosa over to get them. Retrieving the microphone from the ground, his raspy voice again bellows over the loudspeaker. "Yeah, you kids? I've got another two hundred mini-posters for the show here. Put 'em up around town this afternoon. Make sure you stick 'em where the tourists go, since they're all here for the big holiday parade weekend. Got to get butts in these seats tonight if anybody thinks they're gettin' a paycheck later. Got that?"

"Sí, Mr. Stryker. We will go to Michigan Avenue." Rico grabs a stack of flyers from Rosa. He slides them inside his leather jacket for safekeeping. His twin appears to say something to him, but Rico only shrugs and turns back to El Capitán. Annoyed, Rosa stalks off. She sweeps her long dark hair over one shoulder and accepts a bottle of water from a crew member.

Maxzyne watches Rico tap El Capitán on one knee. The horse makes a graceful bow again. With a nod, Rico signals the horse to rise and rewards him with a pat on his muscular chest. From his pants pocket, he discreetly slips him a few carrot bits as a reward. *He really seems to care about horses. Just like Caesar. Hmm. I bet that's what Rosa was asking him.*

The loudspeaker shrieks again, startling everyone. From the far end of the arena, Mr. Stryker waves. "Okay! Schedule change. Next up: Dance of the Clowns. Luis, I want you to . . ." His gravelly voice is suddenly drowned out by a passing fire truck on the street outside. Despite the loud wail of the siren, four show riders take their positions around the ring. The men wait as the blasting horn and loud sirens pass. Once the noise fades, a merry tune is piped into the arena. On cue, the men on horseback leap from their saddles. They tumble and leap playfully from one horse to another, all in time to the music.

Maxzyne is captivated until she spots Rico leading El Capitán toward the stable doors behind her. *Uh-oh, he must be taking him to the stall. I better get back before he sees me.*

The loudspeaker crackles to life again. "Like I was saying, guys. Luis, we need more cartwheels and handstands during this number. Give me a breakout move when the lights change and . . ."

The sound of splintering wood and thrashing behind Maxzyne is terrifying. She forgets everything, including the need to stay hidden, and scurries to safety. Goosebumps rise on her arms and neck as a streak of black mane, tail, and hooves pounds past her.

Caesar! She gasps as the frightened horse races toward the ring. Certain that he is a danger to anything in his path, she screams. "Stop! Whoa, Caesar!" Despite her cries, the horse dashes past a shocked Rico. The panicked horse streaks toward El Capitán, who neighs a loud warning. Caesar enters the ring, running and kicking wildly. The other riders shout and swarm over the rails. They wave their hats and call out to the distressed runaway horse. There is no stopping him as he stomps, bucks, and snorts. His nostrils flare and his eyes roll behind the leather blinders.

Maxzyne's heart sinks. From across the aisle of bleachers, she looks at Rico, knowing she's caught. He ignores her, quickly securing El Capitán's reins to a nearby railing. She watches, nervously twisting and pulling a red barrette loose from a braid near her cheek. The hard plastic reaches her mouth. Without a second thought, she bites hard on the clip, fearing the worst as Rico rushes into the ring to stop the crazy horse.

5

Rico to the Rescue

W HOA, AMIGO! Stop, Caesar! Whoa!" With great bravado, Rico waves his hands at the horse. He makes more strange noises with his tongue, but there is no calming the spooked animal.

"What the heck's going on here?" Furious at the intrusion, the boss tears his cap from his head, throws it down, and angrily stomps his foot. "How'd this crazy horse get in here? Ricardo, do something before your son gets killed!"

From the sidelines, a tall, slender man with a long ponytail trailing beneath his black suede hat races into the ring. He expertly rides a muscular gray stallion the color of storm clouds. Slowly, he unwinds a length of braided leather rope from his belt. All eyes are on him as he edges closer to Caesar. He never takes his eyes off the runaway horse as he raises the lasso above his own head. The rope swings in a wide arc. Maxzyne holds her breath. Everyone in the arena shouts when Ricardo easily drops the lasso over Caesar's thrashing head. The skilled horseman leans into the rope and pulls hard.

"That's it! Show 'im who's boss, Ricardo!" Mr. Stryker picks up his cap and waves it at Ricardo. Before putting it back on his head, he smacks it on his thigh several times, transferring the dust to his trousers.

But the crackling loudspeaker only enrages the panicked horse. Caesar strains and thrashes against the rope around his neck. Dust swirls as he bucks and kicks dangerously close to the edge of the metal bleachers. Horrified, Maxzyne drops the barrette as she clamps a hand over her mouth. *Please don't let him get hurt.* She watches Ricardo draw the line taut. He slows his own horse, but Caesar's heaving strength nearly jerks the rope from his hands. Sensing the danger, two other men leap from their horses to help. They each grab the rope with gloved hands, barely avoiding Caesar's kicking hooves.

"¡Basta, ya! (Whoa!) ¡Basta, ya!" The men are strong, but Caesar drags them along for several yards as they shout. Finally, the spooked horse is stopped. The other riders rush in from the sidelines. They quickly form a ring around Caesar and block him inside.

The angry boss pushes through the group. He stares at the trembling, panting horse. "Somebody better tell me what's going on here!" he yells. "Where'd this horse come from?" There is an uncomfortable silence. Not getting an answer, he turns and points at Maxzyne. "You, get over here!"

She bites her lower lip, afraid to look at Rico. There is a murmur of Spanish as she slowly walks around the bleachers and into the ring.

Rosa stands next to Rico and taps his shin with the pointy toe of her boot. "¡*Ahora estamos en problemas, Rico!*" (Now we're in trouble, Rico!)

Ricardo pulls the brim of his black hat away from his face and gives Rico a sharp look. "Son, what have you done? ¿*Has traido problemas a nuestra familia?*" (Have you brought trouble to our family?) The older man wipes his tanned forehead with the black-and-white bandanna knotted around his neck. "You make trouble for Mr. Stryker?" Rico's father shakes his head and glances at the boss. Rico just crosses his arms and glares at Rosa.

The inside of Maxzyne's bottom lip starts to bleed where she is biting the red hair clip. She quickly refastens the barrette to the braid, takes a deep breath, and dares to speak. "L-l-look, we were just trying to help! Caesar scares easily, and we thought maybe we could . . ."

"Stop right there, girly. 'Maybe we could' what? Break my arena doors?" Mr. Stryker points to the splintered door behind them. "Destroy a stall? Spook the other horses? Injure those trying to stop him?" His growly voice bellows, "Do you know what my insurance costs are already, Miss Maybe-We-Could?"

Around her, the crowd murmurs under their breath. "It was me, boss." Rico straightens his shoulders and looks directly at the irate man. "The horse was *un fugitivo* (a runaway). I made him calm and we were going to . . ."

"You're going to, all right," the burly man interrupts with a sneer. He jabs a thumb in Rico's chest. "You're going to lose a paycheck for the damage you've caused!"

Ricardo steps forward, his dark eyes flashing. "But Mr. Stryker. My boy means no harm!" The worried man hands Caesar's reins to the boss.

Rico chimes in. "*¡Sí, jefe!*" (Yes, boss!)

His father nods and continues in a softer voice. "We work it out, ¿sí? The Callea family?" He gives Rico a grim look. "We fix a mistake."

Stryker puts his hands on his hips. Between bristly, whiskered cheeks, his lips stretch into a smirk. "Well, here's what you *are* going to do." He points to the ring. "First, finish rehearsal."

Ricardo nods solemnly.

Mr. Stryker raises two fingers. "Second, you repair that door and the stall that I know must be wrecked." With a scowl, he jerks his head in the direction of the stable. He raises a third finger and turns his steely eyes to Rico. "And *you* are going to triple tie that crazy horse away from all the other horses." He throws the reins at the young boy, who catches them easily. "Oh—and Luis?" Another dark-haired man wearing a yellow bandanna around his neck steps forward.

"¿Sí, jefe?" he asks nervously.

"Luis, I need you to find out exactly *who* owns this horse! I think I'll sue 'em for damages."

Ricardo shakes his head. "We want no trouble, sir. We fix everything."

The boss glowers at Maxzyne. "Yeah? Well, there's one thing I'm about to fix, folks. I'm calling the police about this trespasser!"

Maxzyne is aghast. *Is he talking about me?* There is no time to run. Instead, two thick arms with hairy wrists grab her. Mr. Stryker is quick for such a big man. His bruising grip pinches her elbow.

"Ouch! You're hurting me," she shrieks. "I didn't do anything!"

"Tell it to the cops, missy." He leans into her face. "Once they write their report, maybe I sue *you* for damages."

She tries to duck sideways but can't escape. He notices her dusty khaki pants and upturned polo shirt with the school monogram beneath the borrowed leather jacket. His bushy salt-and-pepper eyebrows rise. "A private school brat like you must have parents who'll cough up some cash," he sneers. His fat pink lips turn up at the corners. Somehow, it makes his grizzled beard and mustache seem to twitch.

Ricardo looks worried. "Let her go, Mr. Stryker. I'll see there's no more trouble."

"Who's the boss here, anyway?" the angry man roars. His face and neck streak red as he glowers at Ricardo. "I'll fire the whole Callea family without pay! Cross me again? Your kids have talent, but everybody knows I'm doing a favor letting 'em work here. *Off* the books." He gives Ricardo a meaningful look. "I don't ask questions, but they don't look sixteen to me."

Ricardo's face pales and his shoulders slump. All around him there is a soft muttering of Spanish. He shakes his head and the other performers melt away. Mr. Stryker yanks Maxzyne by the arm. "C'mon, kid. I've got a call to make." He smirks at Ricardo, Rico, and Rosa.

Suddenly, Rico springs into action. Quick as lightning, he scrambles into Caesar's saddle and rides to Maxzyne. He digs into Stryker's arm with the pointy toe of his dusty leather boot. The pressure forces the man to drop Maxzyne's arm.

"Just what do you think you're doin', kid?" the stunned boss hollers. Maxzyne darts around to the other side of the horse, trying to get as far as possible from the man.

"¡Rápido! We go now, High-rise!" Rico reaches low and offers his hand. She stands on her tiptoes and lets him pull her up with one strong hand. Elated to be free of Mr. Stryker, she scrambles up and into the saddle.

Rico makes a trilling noise with his tongue, giving a series of quick calls. Caesar's ears prick and he trots forward. Maxzyne holds on to the saddle horn with both hands as her feet swing wildly. She is barely able to keep her balance in the saddle. Rico steadies her with his free hand as he expertly guides Caesar through the splintered stable door.

"Rico, you are loco!" Rosa calls after him. "We can't lose this job. We need the money!"

"You're gonna regret this, boy!" screams Mr. Stryker. "And you, too, missy!" Furious, throws his cap after the fleeing horse and riders. Forced to lean forward in order to keep her balance, Maxzyne is relieved when she can no longer see the enraged red-faced man.

"Sí, son, think of what you are doing." Ricardo's plea drifts away as Caesar's hooves pound through the stall corridor. The other horses are startled. Behind closed doors, they neigh their surprise and rustle in agitation. The restless animal sounds fade as the trio bursts through the huge stone archway and into the damp, crisp air of a fading afternoon.

6

Trust

MAXZYNE CAN HARDLY SEE past her own braids. The entwined strands, locked into place with red and white barrettes, bounce across her face in time to Caesar's trotting hooves. Thankfully, the street is deserted. The horse seems to have calmed under Rico's direction and expert hands. She feels the tension in her own shoulders relax a bit as she listens to the soft-spoken commands given by the young horseman. For the moment, there is no need for a gentle flick of the whip.

"That's it, amigo," he croons. "You are in charge, but I lead."

"Uh, Rico?" She squirms in the saddle. Her neck twists as she tries to see his face. When she nearly loses her balance on the unstable perch, she decides to keep both hands on the saddle horn instead. "Just wondering—do you know where we're going?"

There is a long pause as Rico carefully considers her question. "Someplace where people—and horses—matter. ¿Sí, Caesar?" He guides the horse toward the left lane of the quiet intersection on a tree-lined street.

Caesar whinnies in response.

Hmm. It's as if he understands Caesar. But how can he? I've got the magic hat. She slides the canvas backpack strap higher on her shoulder. *How else does he do it, though?* Maxzyne can't answer these questions and shrugs in agreement with their destination. "Okay, that's cool." A light gust of wind blows a damp chill down her neck. With a shiver, she pulls up her shirt collar. *Good thing I borrowed this jacket.* She sits up straight, grateful for and yet uncomfortably aware of Rico's body heat as he sits so close behind her in the saddle. She decides it's best to relax into the rhythm of the horse. "So where exactly do people and horses matter in this town? I mean, if I know what the plan is, I can help."

"Help, High-rise?" His voice rises. "I made a plan, *¿recuerdas?* (remember?) Now we have trouble." With an exasperated flick of the riding crop, he slows Caesar down to a gentle trot.

"Hey, no fair playing the blame game. If you recall, Caesar was the one who went crazy on us!" she calls over her shoulder.

"Sí. Because we 'bring him to the theatre!' Now *mi familia* (my family) has big trouble. Maybe we lose our jobs and paychecks."

Indignant at his accusation, she arches her back. "Brain freeze! I was just trying to help the horse. You're the one who stopped him!" she hisses. "Besides, kids aren't even s'posed to have jobs." Defiant, she turns sideways, but nearly loses her balance again. She quickly faces forward again. "Don't you even go to school?" she huffs.

For what seems like a very long time, Rico remains silent.

"Well? Talk much?" she taunts. Behind her, he responds with a derisive snort.

"Rosa and I go to school in the morning." His voice is harsh. "The school calls it a 'newcomer' program, but the other kids call it the 'dummy' program." From where he sits behind her, she can feel him shrug his shoulders as if he doesn't care. "Sí, English is not our language," he scoffs. "So we are slow. *Estúpidos.* (Stupid) Let them think it." Annoyed, he kicks his feet out of the stirrups. Maxzyne just nods and waits for him to continue. "And Miss Gomez, she comes to our apartment *todos los sábados* (every Saturday) to help us."

She interrupts. "Is that every Saturday?"

He gives a frustrated sigh. "Sí. So we can be caught. Er, catch up." He leans toward her in the saddle. "You know *español* (Spanish)?"

"Not like you." She shakes her head and the plastic barrettes rattle. "I just started taking Spanish this year," she explains. "Besides, your English is good." She chuckles. "Lots better than my Spanish. You don't need that dummy program."

Rico scoffs. "Tell that to *la escuela* (the school). Rosa and me, we know what we need to know. We know horses! ¡Sí! Los caballos. What else matters, eh, Caesar?" He twists the reins tighter in his sturdy brown hand.

"Yeah," she agrees, "you know an awful lot." A wry, lopsided grin crosses her face. "I saw you both practicing back there. Pretty cool, but scary. I thought somebody might die, 'specially Rosa! Those daredevil moves? Standing on horseback? Yikes! On one leg, even. Where'd you learn that stuff, anyway?" Admiration creeps into her voice. "Not to mention, don't you get, um, scared? You know, riding so fast in circles?" She pauses to look at the ground and shudders. She can't see him grin behind her. "Seriously, Rico. I can't believe Rosa didn't fall. I'd be in a body cast, for sure."

Rico coughs into his shoulder, trying to stifle a laugh. "*Gaucho*s (skilled horse riders) are not scared of los caballos," he scoffs. He steers Caesar down a narrow side street. "It is in our bones and blood to ride a horse. Man and beast, we are as one." The young horseman sees a deserted parking lot on the right. He pulls on the reins. Caesar stops on the cracked asphalt that adjoins a vacant, boarded-up building. "Rosa?" He shrugs. "She is a girl." Maxzyne can hear the edge creep back in his voice but doesn't say anything. "Like me, she wants only to be with the horses. Our *madre* (mother) was not happy with her choice." He raises his arms in a dramatic shrug. "We are twins." His voice sounds far away. "Born to ride horses."

"So you're kinda like a cowboy?"

He playfully pokes her in the shoulder blade. "Sí, but no cows in Chicago." She gives him a backward elbow, but he catches it just in time. "Right, just steak." They both chuckle at his joke for a minute and fall silent. She glances at the vacant building.

"Okay, city gaucho. You want to help save a carriage horse, right? Well, we gotta have a plan. My dad always says, 'You need an edge to overcome uncertainty.' And things are kind of uncertain right now, don't you think?"

Rico inhales deeply. She waits as the air drains from his lips, his breath warm on her neck, which annoys her. Impatient to hear his plan, she whips around. Several of her braids catch him in the face. He leans back in the saddle, crying out. "I'm still thinking, High-rise!"

"Yeah, well, let's think faster *together*, huh?" She screws up her face and closes her eyes. "So I'm thinking the only place that cares about people *and* horses is— drumroll, please—the Chicago Mounted Police," she declares. "And there's a . . ."

Behind her, Rico positively jumps in the saddle. "No! No *policía* (police)."

"Whoa, cowboy!" She motions a braking gesture with both hands. "For someone so great on a horse, you sure are a scaredy-cat!" She is quick to qualify her statement. "I mean, about city stuff. Seriously, the mounted police are great. Even better? I'm friends with one. I always see Officer Logan riding through Millennium Park. Or on Michigan Avenue sometimes, but mostly during festivals and parades. He's really nice."

"No!" Behind her, Rico violently shakes his head.

Undaunted, she continues. "He even lets us pet his horse, Ace. Or take photos. You'll really like him." She throws out her hands as if it were obvious.

"Sí, *pero ningún policía.* (Yes, but no police.) Our family does not want trouble."

"But the police can help us," she insists.

Rico twirls the reins in his hand. "Gauchos have no use for police. Not now. Not ever. Rosa, she is right; we need this job. It is the only way we can get back to my country. We owe the bank money for our *estancia* (ranch)." He sighs, his voice wistful. "It was our family home for many generations. Leaving it felt like a natural law was broken."

Maxzyne watches Caesar nibble a mound of weeds growing through the cracked asphalt. "You mean you might lose your home?"

"Sí. Not much work for gauchos these days. So we come to America." He watches Caesar graze. "My

Uncle Luis said there was work for my parents on a big farm in Texas." He sighs, remembering. "The trip was long. Trains. Buses. Everyone with backpacks and big dreams of life in America. But for me, it was no dream. I was sad to cross the border."

Maxzyne is perplexed. "Sad? Why?"

Behind her, Rico's voice bristles. "Showing papers, questions, government officials, la policía search us as if we are thieves," he complains, ticking off the items on his fingers. "Gauchos don't believe in borders. Everything should be open and free. Like it was in my country." His voice turns hard. "Before the banks made fences with their rules. That's why we had to leave."

"Yeah? Where's that?"

"Uruguay in South America. Far away." His voice drops to a whisper. "The best place on earth."

"But now you're here. It's all good, right?"

"Good for picking vegetables in Texas, sí. Moving from farm to farm, sí." He juggles the loose reins from hand to hand. "Working for a jefe like Mr. Stryker? Feels like we're still stuck between fences, High-rise. Only now we're on *this* side of the border."

"Hmmph!" She shrugs, annoyed. "Well, it's a free country, y'know. You can go home if you don't like it." Rico gives a loud snort, making Caesar prick his ears at him. "I told you. We have to pay the bank for our house and land by the end of the year or it's lost forever."

"Oh. Yeah." Feeling his sadness, she changes the subject. "Well, what about Texas? That seems like a good place for a horse-loving cowboy, right?"

He winds the reins tighter around his wrist, lost in reflection. "During the summer, no school, so we pick vegetables all day. After, I sneak to the barn. Just to be near los caballos. My earth spirits." His voice turns wistful again. "I am home when I ride them, feed them, talk to them."

Maxzyne shifts in her perch, puzzled. *What's this about horse talk? I'm the one with the hat!* She keeps her secret to herself as Rico's voice drops to a soft whisper. "The work is hard, but we make money, and *Papá* (Dad) is happy. He and my uncle count el dinero every night. We keep moving to the next crop, every week a new farm. But there is still not enough to give the bank for our home." Suddenly, his voice brightens. "But one day—the best day—something *bueno* (good) happens. No! *¡Muy bueno!*" (Very good!) He flicks the whip in the air.

Maxzyne wriggles in her seat, growing impatient. "Yay, don't keep me in suspense. Spill the beans." Rico yanks one of her back braids. "Ouch!" she wails.

He yanks again, enjoying his storytelling power. "Keep your spurs on, High-rise."

"Owww! If I had spurs, I know who I would use them on!" She ducks her head, protecting her braids with both hands.

Rico taps the handle of the riding crop on her shoulder. "If you must know, that was the day Papá let Rosa and me enter a rodeo contest in Texas."

"Cool," she marvels then twists in the saddle to see him. "Though I've never been to a rodeo before." She leans over and strokes Caesar's dark mane. "True confession, Rico. Until today, the only horse I ever knew was Officer Logan's. Now I'm riding one."

Rico nods. She glances back to see a wide grin cross his face. "Like trying to lasso the wind, riding a new horse. Rosa and I got our chance at the rodeo." He snaps his fingers. "First, we borrowed a horse. A horse I cared for when it was sick. I knew him well, so man and beast were as one."

"Huh?" Maxzyne is confused. "What's that mean?"

"The horse gave me his trust. And Rosa? She gave us both her trust, so we won."

Maxzyne claps her hands, bouncing in the saddle. "Woo-hoo! First place!" She shifts forward, looking puzzled. "Won what, exactly, a race?"

"Uh, no. Best horse duo. Youth Division." He twirls the reins in his hands, remembering. "It was a good day. Our moves were simple then, not like now." His voice grows thoughtful. "But it was not skill that won." He shakes his head emphatically, a dark shock of hair falling across his face.

"What do you mean, Rico? You won fair and square, right?"

He flips his hair from his eyes with an impatient hand. "¡Sí! Of course. But trust won the contest. When we ride a horse, we trust as a team. We think, we move, we *are* a team."

Maxzyne nods. "I guess having a twin like Rosa is pretty special. Always being a team. Sure wish I had one sometimes," she whispers. "But then there'd be double trouble, I s'pose."

"Sí, we share our mother's breath. We are tied together—as one with the horses and with each other." He gives a rueful chuckle. "Maybe too much. Like when she says she was born first and knows best," he scoffs.

Maxzyne straightens up and throws her shoulders back, hands on her hips. "Uh, well, maybe Rosa does," she proclaims. "Girls usually do know best." She scoots forward in the saddle, but there is no jab in the back or jerk of her braids from behind. Rico remains silent.

"Okay," she offers, uncomfortable with his silence. She throws her right leg over the saddle horn, letting both legs dangle restlessly as she confides, "I don't actually have a brother or sister. So I missed that teamwork thing. Except in soccer, of course. And even then, you're only as good as your last score. Besides, everybody on the team gets a trophy at the end of the season. It's no big deal."

"To win the rodeo was a big deal, High-rise. The prize money was a big deal," he insists. "It gave us hope we could save our home and one day return there."

As if in agreement, Caesar stops snuffling weeds and whinnies. *Did he just say when the carriage tourists tipped big, he got extra oats to eat?* Distracted, she listens for another whinny from Caesar, but he continues to munch on green shoots growing through the cracked asphalt. Just having the magic hat in her possession gives her fleeting impressions about the horse, but Rico doesn't seem to notice anything.

She returns to her questions. "Then you came to Chicago, right? To be in the show here?"

Rico shakes his head. "First, we did carnivals. Mr. Stryker saw us on the circuit. He offered us a job. *Mamá* (Mom) wanted to put down, er, *las raíces.*" He frowns, trying to find the right word in English.

"Hmm. You mean, 'roots'? Put down roots?" she adds helpfully.

"Sí, that's it. Roots. *Mamá* wants us to stay in one place so Rosa and I can spend more time in school. To make a better life for us."

"No way kids get out of school in this country, huh?" Recalling her own trouble at school, her conscience pricks. She ignores it, instead nodding for Rico to continue.

"So Mr. Stryker made a deal with us. We ride in his show and he gives us a part of ticket sales. But we need money fast, right? So Rosa and I pretend we are *estúpidos* in school to stay in the early morning 'dummy program.' That way we can practice new moves in the afternoon and ride in more shows." He lets his chin drop, unable to meet Maxzyne's gaze. "It was the boss's idea. Mamá does not know." He shrugs. "Papá and Uncle Luis say we almost have enough dinero to go back to Uruguay. Enough to pay the bank what we owe for our estancia." He throws out his hands, nearly dropping the reins, but catches them just in time. "*Hasta entonces* (Until then), what can we do?" He gives a sarcastic growl. "We just needed a little more cash. By Christmas we might have saved enough, but after the damage to the stall and barn and then . . ." his voice trails off.

Caesar's ears prick their way as he snuffles among the weeds. He seems content to be on a quiet street with the two young riders. Maxzyne and Rico listen to him, each lost in their own thoughts. Rico is the first to speak. "It is good to be on a horse again, but I miss *las pampas* (the plains)." He sighs.

"Well, you won't lose your job, will you? I mean, Mr. Stryker wouldn't fire you just for helping Caesar. Nobody's that mean, right?" They are startled when Caesar suddenly sneezes, making them both laugh.

"*¡Salud!*" (Bless you!) Rico calls out to the horse. He pats Caesar on the flank before answering her question. "Maybe. *Peor* (Worse), he calls la policía, and they ask too many questions about school." He throws his hands out dramatically. "The other kids make fun of us, but Rosa and I work hard to be dummies." He lowers his arms, grinning when Maxzyne giggles. His eyes grow thoughtful when he strokes Caesar again. "Anyway, I had to save this horse. For a gaucho, the horse *always* comes first."

"Even before family?"

"A horse *is* family."

He reaches past her and rubs Caesar lightly between the ears. To their surprise, the horse lowers himself to the ground, bending his two front legs in a graceful bow. Stunned, the two easily slide from their high perch in the saddle to the ground. Rico laughs. Smiling, he lets the reins fall from his hands.

"This horse is no taxi. Caesar, show me more, amigo." He taps the horse lightly on the neck. His grin widens as the horse rises to stand on all fours.

"You mean he does tricks?"

"Maybe." The boy's eyes sparkle. "I saw horses like him in the carnival. Watching them, I learned the horse code."

"You mean signals? To show them what trick to do?"

"Sí. We use it for our horses in the show. But some signs are com—er . . ."

"Complicated?" she offers helpfully.

"Sí, complicated." He turns back to the horse. "Caesar, we do a test. Maybe you are a show horse, eh? A prince in disguise."

"Oooh, like in a fairytale," Maxzyne gushes.

Rico smirks. "Sí, but without the kiss, High-rise."

Her cheeks grow warm. "Who said anything about kissing, anyway? You're just giving him a test," she snaps. *Geez! Boys should come with the warning: will make fun of anything a girl says or does at all times.* "Hummph!" she snorts, her nostrils flaring.

Rico ignores her irritation. Instead, he gently taps Caesar's two front legs with the riding crop. Amazed, they watch the horse come to life. He lifts his hooves in a jaunty dance, head erect, tail held high. Maxzyne stares, her mouth wide open.

Rico grins at her. "Careful, High-rise. You'll catch flies like that!"

Her jaw snaps shut. Despite her annoyance with him, she can't hide her wonder. "B-b-but that's so cool! You made him dance, Rico. Look—he's a different horse, isn't he? With his own secret dance language."

With a nod, Rico taps Caesar's knees again. Right on cue, the horse stands still on the asphalt. Then he taps the horse's left ear. Caesar turns in a circle to the left. When Rico taps the right ear, the horse easily makes another circle to the right.

"*Inteligente.* (Intelligent.) His eyes. I knew it." Rico taps Caesar twice on the chest. The horse lowers himself to a seated position on the cracked asphalt. "Someone trained you well, eh, amigo?"

Caesar nickers and waits patiently for the next command. The boy taps the horse under his long chin.

Slowly, Caesar rises. His curious eyes follow the young horseman's hands. Finally, Rico reaches into his pants pocket and retrieves a plastic zip bag of carrot chips. He offers several carrots to the horse. Caesar draws back his lips, showing his big yellow teeth and dark tongue. Rico is careful to let him eat from the flat of his palm.

In her excitement, Maxzyne's words tumble in a rush. "I've never met anyone like you before, Rico." She raises one hand to tick off items on her fingers. "One: you know horses. Like, you know so much about them, it's almost spooky. Two: we need to save *this horse*. And three: you need to keep your job riding horses." Unconcerned, Caesar noisily crunches carrots.

Rico carefully stows the zip bag in his pocket. The horse sniffs his jacket pocket, disappointed. He turns to look at Maxzyne with pleading eyes. She holds up her empty hands in front of his snout. "Sorry, buddy. I'm fresh out!" With a derisive snort, the horse returns to sniffing a weedy patch in the asphalt.

"Listen, Rico. I think you have to trust people sometimes. And I trust Officer Logan a lot. I mean, really." The boy ignores her and retrieves the leather reins. "Hey, are you even listening to me?" she demands.

"Save your breath, High-rise." He stands, arms folded across his chest, a steely glint in his eyes.

"No! Not till you tell me you're gonna help save this horse, cowboy!" To prove she means business, she folds her own arms across her chest. It isn't hard to glare back at him. "You said you and Rosa won that rodeo because you were a team, remember?"

Rico gives her a skeptical nod.

"Well, looks like I'm the only team you've got right now. And he needs us." She points at the horse and waits. Caesar whinnies and bobs his head as if in agreement. "See? Even he wants us to be his team." She strokes the horse's cheek. "We won't let you down, buddy," she croons.

Finally, Rico nods, letting his arms fall to his sides. "We are not the 'A Team,'" he retorts.

She ignores his taunt and lets her own arms drop. "So like I was saying . . . once I got stranded in a crowd at Navy Pier during the fireworks. Next thing I knew, Officer Logan and his horse, Ace, helped me get back to my parents." She feels herself starting to blush. "I was only six, so it was a big deal." Suddenly self-conscious, she nervously fiddles with one of her barrettes. "Anyway, my parents took me to see Ace later. I gave him some apples." She exhales, in a hurry to make her point. "So that's why I know Officer Logan would help Caesar. Really."

From behind the horse they hear a splat. Caesar takes several steps forward, steering clear of the droppings. The smell of fresh horse manure drifts up from the pavement. Maxzyne holds her nose and points at the pile. She has the distinct impression that Caesar is embarrassed. *Did he just say "Excuse me?"*

"Besides, it's getting kind of stinky here . . ."

Rico swings the reins in his right hand. "This Officer Logan—you think he will do the right thing for Caesar?" He looks doubtful. "This horse must not work in the streets. It will kill him." He leans forward and strokes Caesar's cheek with the back of his hand. Maxzyne hears him whisper, "You are too good for that, amigo. Too proud." The graceful animal raises his head and nickers in response, his fat dark lips vibrating.

She can't contain her curiosity. "Do you think he understands us, Rico? I mean, it's not like horses can talk, I s'pose. It just seems he knows what we're saying and wants to tell us stuff . . ." she trails off, not wanting to appear foolish.

"Every gaucho knows horses can't talk, Highrise. But with time and experience, there is no need for words, eh, Caesar?" He grins at the horse before turning back to Maxzyne and offering his arm. She rolls her eyes in exasperation. *Oh yeah? Rico thinks he knows so much. Well, I'm definitely not telling him about the magic hat!*

"If you think Officer Logan won't ask too many questions about school and work, we'll ask him to help. And now, ladies first."

With a very unladylike grunt, Maxzyne pulls herself up into the saddle. In a flash, she tries to tug the reins away from Rico. Not to be outdone, he scrambles up beside her. He gives her a smug look, tightly holding the reins. With a low whistle, he lightly taps the riding crop on the horse's strong shoulders. The unlikely trio moves back to the sidewalk as Caesar trots quickly past the abandoned lot and derelict building.

Still in control, Rico flicks the reins. "I trust you to show the way, High-rise. But this horse? He trusts only a gaucho. He told me."

7

Officer Logan

THE RIDERS SETTLE into a companionable silence. Rico guides the trotting horse south along the deserted lakefront, according to Maxzyne's directions. Thirty minutes later, Caesar slows to a walk. They enter a long, circular drive flanked by barren flowerbeds covered with mulch. Maxzyne points to their destination. "This used to be an exclusive country club, I guess. But don't worry. It's not private anymore—anyone can reserve it for parties and stuff now. My parents took me to a wedding here last summer."

Rico stares at the stately brick building. Long rows of windows march across the front. Two matching towers guard each end. The historic building looks bleak in the late afternoon light. The grounds, normally bursting with seasonal flowers and handsome trees, look stark and bare. As they draw close to the main entrance, she points to one side. "This way, guys. The stables are in back."

Rico guides the horse along a well-worn path. When they turn a corner, he is surprised to see a fenced area. Beyond the fence, acres of open parkland beckon. His eyes sweep across the gently rolling landscape, the grass brittle and brown until spring. To the east, the hard earth becomes a ridge overlooking Lake Michigan. The water looks silver from their vantage point.

Maxzyne is surprised when Rico suddenly punches the air with his fist. "¡Sí! This is what a horse needs. Room to run. Fresh air to breathe. Maybe you are right about la policía, High-rise. They do care about horses here."

There is a sudden thrum of hooves on the packed earth near the stable entrance. Rico pulls Caesar's reins taut. They stop and wait. Seconds later, a mounted policeman riding on a proud brown gelding appears. Puzzled, he pulls his horse beside them.

"Hey! You kids can't ride without helmets." He taps his own black hard hat. A silver shield shines on the crown above his forehead. "That's not good horse safety, you know. Where's your trainer?"

Go figure. As much as I love hats, I'm caught not wearing one when I should be. Maxzyne forces her cold lips into a bright smile.

"Uh, sir? We were just going to see Officer Logan, actually. We'll go straight to the barn, if that's okay?"

"Sí, Officer. You know Ace, his horse?" Rico adds, giving their story a whiff of authenticity. The man nods. "We bring him treats." Rico slides the plastic bag of carrots from his pants pocket. With a bold grin, he waves it at the officer.

"Well, okay. But make sure Logan gives you some practice helmets. We can't have kids falling on their heads around here. Gives everyone a headache— especially the chief!" With a snap of the reins, the horse and uniformed rider trot toward the fence and disappear into the open parkland.

"Gauchos do not fall on their heads," Rico mutters.

Maxzyne nudges him with her elbow. "Shhhh," she hisses. "Around here, you need a helmet just riding a bike. Let's get to the barn already. Nice touch, bringing up the carrots, amigo. Hope Caesar doesn't mind sharing."

Rico makes that funny noise with his tongue and Caesar's ears prick as he moves forward. At the entrance, the two decide to jump down from the horse. "Ladies before gentlemen," Maxzyne chirps, as sliding off the saddle. On the ground again, she feels small beside the big horse.

Graceful as a cat leaping from a tree branch, Rico jumps down beside her. With a firm grip on the reins, he leads Caesar into the airy interior of the mounted police stables. The now-familiar smell of manure, hay, and leather greets them as they enter. Under the high ceiling, long bright lights hang, reflecting the whitewashed walls around them. In the center is a practice ring of soft, dark earth. On the far end, a delighted horse rolls on his back, hooves high in the air.

Maxzyne recognizes the man hanging over the railing. He smiles and chats with the horse. "That's it, Ace. Put your feet up and enjoy yourself. It's gonna be crazy out there on Michigan Avenue tonight."

Rico smiles at the mahogany horse cavorting in the ring. "This is a happy horse," he whispers excitedly in Maxzyne's ear. "Maybe you are right about la policía."

"Team Maxzyne is always right," she whispers, resisting the urge to stick out her tongue. "Now just let me do the talking."

"Nobody does that better than you, X, Z, and Y," he quietly taunts, ducking the jab she tries to give with her elbow.

The horse and riders walk toward Officer Logan, finally stopping a respectful distance from the man. Maxzyne clears her throat. "Ah . . . hem! Um, Officer Logan?" The lanky police officer straightens up, pushing away from the railing. He looks curiously at Maxzyne as she strides toward him. *Breathe.* She smiles and waves. "It's Maxzyne, sir. Remember? You and Ace saved me that time at Navy Pier? And I was out here for a wedding last summer with my parents. You took my photo with Ace."

The man's warm brown eyes crinkle around the edges. His dark face relaxes under his wide-brimmed hat when he breaks into a smile. "How could I forget Maxzyne Merriweather? I didn't expect to see you here today. What brings you to our stomping grounds?" He turns and raps on the railing. The horse quickly stops snuffling and rolling on the ground. "Ace, buddy. Mind your manners. Look who's here—one of your—*our*—success stories. Get up here and say hello to Maxzyne."

The big horse rises with a graceful unfolding of his long legs. Once standing, he snorts and shimmies to shake the dust from his mane. Rico sneaks Maxzyne a carrot from his bag. She grins. Holding it up to the horse's velvety nose, she offers it, careful to leave it flat in the palm of her hand. It tickles when his mouth opens and his gentle lips reach for it. *Wouldn't want those big teeth taking off a finger, that's for sure.* Caesar suddenly whinnies, annoyed at the attention being paid to the other horse.

"Sí, amigo. One for you too." Rico offers him a carrot chunk and turns to the policeman. "Sir, do you mind if this horse drinks some water from over there?" He points at a long trough hanging from the wall nearby.

Officer Logan nods but looks perplexed. "Sure. Horses need to hydrate just like people." He watches Rico lead Caesar to the water trough. The horse eagerly dips his head and slurps with his long tongue.

"So who's this, Maxzyne? I didn't know you were interested in learning to ride our four-legged friends."

He jerks his thumb toward Rico. "But your pal over there certainly seems comfortable with them."

"Oh, yeah, he's a natural." She waves, signaling Rico to return. "But, uh, Officer Logan?" She lowers her voice. "See, there's something we need your help with, sir."

"I'm all ears, Miss Merriweather." The officer straightens up, looking tall and official in his navy uniform.

Maxzyne waits until Rico brings Caesar back to where they stand at the railing. "Sir, this horse's name is Caesar, and he ran away from his carriage driver. We found him—well, *I* found him by the school today." She pauses for a second as her conscience pricks. *No need to include anything about being on my way to the principal's office, right?*

She banishes all thoughts of school and continues, "He was going too fast, and a carriage wheel got stuck in the school's sidewalk bike rack. But when I helped get it unstuck, a car honked and that must've scared him." *And definitely don't tell them I was pretending to be a carriage driver.* She feels her face get warm, recalling how she posed in the black silk driver's hat and was then almost hijacked by Caesar.

Rico and the policeman wait patiently for her to continue. "Oh! Anyway, that's when Caesar went crazy, didn't you, boy?" She reaches up to stroke his mane. The horse shakes his head as if disagreeing with her.

Oops, do not use the word "crazy," Maxzyne quickly corrects herself. "I mean, he was spooked by a loud noise and bolted." She gives Caesar a reassuring pat on his muscular chest.

Officer Logan walks around the horse and carefully looks at Caesar. "Well, he seems pretty calm now." He looks at Rico, who nods and gives a small shrug. The policeman tilts his head, waiting for Rico to say something.

The young gaucho's words tumble out, betraying his nervousness. "Sí, er, yes, sir. But you see he is not well cared for, this horse. And because he is stressed, he should not carry tourists on busy streets. He is a danger." Rico frowns and raises his chin in a sudden show of resolve. "No horse should be on the streets, sir. It's bad for the spirit of a horse. And *this* horse? It will kill him." Caesar whinnies and shuffles his hooves restlessly. Maxzyne recalls the sad story she overheard the horse telling Lady Pearl in the stall earlier. She strokes his flank to reassure him.

"Well, my buddy Ace over there, he loves to be out on the streets. But we make sure we only pick horses with the right disposition and then train them for a long time. And reward them too. Isn't that right, Ace?" The regal gelding gives a short whinny and canters once around the ring as if to prove the policeman right.

"Now let's see what we've got here . . ." Officer Logan bends to check Caesar's hooves. His eyes narrow when he sees how worn they are. "Hmm . . . could use some vitamins, given the condition of his feet. He might be getting just enough calories to keep his weight up, but something's not right." He examines the horse's mouth and teeth. "No discharge from mouth and nose—that's good." He pulls back the blinders. "Clear eyes. Okay, let's check your pulse, buddy." He runs his hand along Caesar's jaw, applying light pressure with three fingers. Everyone is quiet while the man moves his lips, counting and looking at his watch.

He drops his hand and nods at Rico.

"Caesar's pulse is high. It could be stress, like you said. And I don't like the look of that scar on his flank either." He turns to Maxzyne. "You didn't happen to see any registration card in the carriage, did you? Company name, anything? We've got rules and regulations for this line of business." He strokes Caesar on the right flank. "Though, if you ask me, the city council could sure make them better."

"Um, it all happened so fast. I didn't think . . ." Maxzyne squeezes her head between her hands. "Snap! I'm not much of a detective, I guess," she stammers.

The officer taps the silver badge on his navy jacket. "That's what I'm here for. Okay, we'll just have to do a little more legwork, but we'll find the owner."

"But the owner does not deserve this horse!" Thunderclouds cross Rico's face.

The policeman looks surprised by his outburst. "That's a bold statement, isn't it?" His tone suddenly grows official. "I didn't quite catch your name, son."

"Rico, sir."

"And how is it you know so much about what's right and wrong for a horse, Rico?" The officer's eyes narrow and he turns to Maxzyne. "Where did you meet this young man? At school?"

Maxzyne doesn't dare look at Rico. "Oh, um, well, there's this horse place—near school," she quickly adds. "They do shows, stuff like that. Rico, he's a ga . . ." She stops herself just in time. "Ga-ga! Just crazy about horses. They're like family to him. He's there every chance he gets." *Whew. Close call.* She'd almost spilled the beans. No point getting Rico in trouble for working when he's too young to have a job.

Officer Logan takes off his black hat with the blue-and-white checkered band and scratches his head. His salt-and-pepper hair is shaved quite close to his head. *He looks so normal without his hat,* Maxzyne thinks. *And his ears stick out. Just like my dad's.*

"Okay. Sounds like you mean well, Rico. I don't think I caught a last name—what was it again?"

Rico swallows nervously. "Uh, Callea, sir."

The officer clears his throat. "Well, then. Mr. Callea and Miss Merriweather, I sure don't like the idea of any horse being mistreated. Or a stressed horse on the run. Or you kids putting yourselves in any danger, despite your good intentions." He claps his broadbrim hat back on his head. "Wait here. I better check and see if he's been reported missing."

The policeman strides away but turns back to call his gelding. "Ace! You better be good and ready for that parade tonight. Go on, get any shenanigans out of your system." The horse snorts and lowers himself down to the ground again. Rico and Maxzyne watch him roll over, joyfully kicking up his hooves in the soft earth.

"Now that horse knows how to chillax, doesn't he, Rico? Caesar, that's what you need."

"I don't know about this, High-rise," Rico worries. "*El agente de policía* (The police officer) seems good to horses. But what if he just follows rules? He might send Caesar back to the streets."

Maxzyne nervously chews the end of a braid. Before Rico can notice, she flings it away from her face. *Disgusting habit. How old am I?*

"Yeah, but we don't have much choice, Rico. He's not *our* horse, remember?"

In a flash, Rico climbs back into the saddle. He leans over and offers her his hand. "I have a bad feeling. Maybe we think of another plan."

Not to be outdone, Maxzyne clambers up beside him. "No time for Plan B, Rico. Besides, my dad always says, 'A handful of patience is worth a bushel of brains.' So just be patient and let *me* be the brains of this rescue operation."

"Sí, pero mi papá says, 'A gaucho cannot change, because wherever he goes, his soul will lead the way.' And my soul leads to this horse."

She grabs the leather reins. "Ha! Not if I've got the reins." The two scuffle, twisting in the saddle. Maxzyne only manages to hang on to the lines by hugging them tightly to her chest.

From the far end of the huge stable, there is a yell. "Hey, you kids! Get down from that horse!" Shocked, they stop fighting over the reins.

"Did you hear me, Maxzyne? Rico?"

Maxzyne is puzzled by Officer Logan's newly stern voice. The policeman's face is tense as he runs toward them, waving a sheet of paper. "A call came in just minutes ago. That horse was reported stolen."

8

Plan B

WITHOUT THINKING, MAXZYNE unfurls the reins and slaps them across Caesar's back. Just as she'd seen Rico do, she digs her heels into the horse's broad sides and yells, "C'mon, Caesar. We're out of here!"

Behind her, Rico makes a clicking noise with his tongue, and the horse takes off. They sail past Officer Logan, who leans in to reach for the reins but comes up empty.

"You can't get away with this, kids. The whole force will be looking for you, mark my words," he bellows. "I'm warning you. Don't go looking for trouble on festival night. I'm coming for you!"

His shouts fade as they burst through the wide stable doors and gallop around the opposite side of the graceful circular drive. The sunset glows overhead, splashing the clouds with red and purple streaks where the sky breaks through. Damp air rises from the nearby lake and creeps under Maxzyne's jacket and shirt collar. Her mind races. *What to do? Which way now?*

Caesar's hooves thunder over the pavement. Realizing what she's just done, she feels goose bumps rise on the back of her neck and shoulders. *Uh-oh. Now I'm REALLY in trouble. The principal's office was bad. But stealing a horse?* Her palms start to sweat and the reins grow slippery in her hands. *Now I'm running from the law . . .*

Behind her, Rico shouts, "Nice job, High-rise. Now, give me the reins, gaucha, before you kill us all!"

Relieved, Maxzyne hands them over. Holding on to the saddle horn with one shaky hand, she points to the foggy moon rising over the silver lake. "We better stay by the water, Rico. The moon will make it bright enough for us to see. They won't think of looking for us out there. It's cold, so there shouldn't be anyone by the lake this time of year." She crosses her fingers in the dark.

Rico leads Caesar toward the shore, letting the horse choose his steps carefully. As the sky slowly melts from pink to gray, the tree trunks glisten in the moonlight, helping the fugitives blend into the shadows. At last they reach the edge of the water where the deserted bike path becomes easier to follow. As the lights twinkle on in the skyscrapers ahead, Maxzyne is glad to be heading in the direction of the city.

"We really need that Plan B now, Rico." There is no sound except the quick trotting of Caesar's hooves beneath them. "Rico? Helllllloooo," she shouts over her shoulder. "We need to figure out our next move." Finally, she turns, jabbing him with her elbow.

"Sí, sí. I hear you," he responds indignantly.

"Well, you didn't say anything!"

"Who needs to talk with you around, High-rise?"

Annoyed, she twists in the saddle. "Hey, I'm your teammate, remember? That means you should respect me."

"And you should respect this view for a minute." Rico throws his arm up and around, as if offering her the rising moon.

"Look at the moon on the lake." He gulps the cold air, exhaling with a wistful sigh. "It looks like la pampa in my country. It goes on forever." His voice cracks a little.

"It is pretty," she agrees. "I've never seen your what'cha call it: la pampa. But I guess Illinois has prairies too. Whenever I see a full moon on the lake from our condo window, it makes me want to catch it."

"I didn't know your building was *that* tall, High-rise," he teases.

Maxzyne bristles at the laughter in his voice. "It's not, silly. I didn't mean *really* catch it. I meant take a picture. Draw or paint it. Save it. That's what artists do, y'know."

"Ah, I see. Like my grandmother. She used to weave a moon symbol into her handmade cloth. I have a scarf she made me for my birthday. It's black with a silver moon. She said it would protect me and my horse." There is a rustling sound as he fumbles inside his jacket for a moment. He gives an elated cry and unfolds a black cotton bandana embroidered with a shining silver moon and delicate white stars. "See? It's always with me." He carefully ties it around his neck.

"If it protects you, is it like magic or something?" Maxzyne asks, remembering the black silk hat in her backpack.

"My grandmother would say so." He snorts. "Me? I don't believe in magic. That's silly talk from elders and long-dead ancestors."

"Yeah, but you did bring it with you," Maxzyne reminds him. "And so far, it's protected you, right?"

"Maybe . . . but I mostly have it to remember her. That's why it's special."

She senses his sadness and tries to keep her voice light. "Well, the moon on the lake is special. Sometimes I like it even better than the Navy Pier fireworks." She points to the right, across the lake where a glittering neon Ferris wheel competes with the moonlight.

Rico claps his hand on his head. "Navy Pier! That's where Mr. Stryker wants me and Rosa to hand out posters about tonight's show. Even if we can save Caesar and I don't lose my job, I'll never be back in time to hand them out. How will folks know to come to the theatre? We'll all lose our jobs because there won't be any money to pay us."

"Well, if you can focus for a second, *I* have an idea."

"Is this more of that 'bushel of brains' talk again? It did not work so good last time," he reminds her. "Your friend, Officer Logan, thinks we stole this horse. Maybe we both go to jail now."

"Hey, try to be positive, okay? I mean, like my dad always says, 'Success is going from failure to failure without losing enthusiasm.'"

"Doesn't your mom ever say anything?" he huffs.

"Of course! She says, 'The sky's the limit. You just have to know how to fly.'"

Rico nods in the dark. "Sí, I like that one." He flicks the reins, spurring Caesar to trot a bit faster.

"Well, she usually says it when I'm drawing instead of doing my homework," Maxzyne admits. This talk about drawing reminds her of how much trouble she is in with her parents and school. Her stomach feels queasy and her throat tightens. She knows her mother must be searching frantically for her at the school. That's even worse than the thought of jail. *But maybe if I can do something positive for this horse . . .*

"So what's the plan, X, Z, and Y? Caesar and I have to approve it. Right, amigo?" He leans forward, making that funny noise with his tongue. In response, the horse trots faster.

"Before I tell you the plan, you need to start calling me by my real name!" she retorts. "Or is that too much to ask, Moonbeam Cowboy?"

"Hey. What's that word you use? Chillax!" He pokes her between the shoulder blades. "So tell me your plan, Team Maxzyne."

"That's better." She holds on to the saddle horn with one hand and pushes several braids away from her eyes with the other. "Okay. Since we can't convince Officer Logan that Caesar needs to be free of his carriage and owner, maybe we need to think outside the box."

"Huh? Outside what box?"

"You know, like outside the ring you ride the horses in. Think bigger. Get it?"

"Ohhh. Sí. So what's this outside-box plan?"

"It's a little more complicated than the first plan, but hear me out. I think we need to try to change things for horses. All horses." She hangs on to the saddle horn with both hands, twisting her neck to see him.

He shakes his head, confused. She shrieks, trying to be heard over the sound of Caesar's clopping hooves. "Imagine if we don't just save Caesar—we save every horse in the city."

Rico pulls on the reins, slowing down the horse. Excited by her new idea, Maxzyne waves her arms at the city skyline. "Last month we learned in civics class at school all about how rules are made in Chicago." She grins and bounces in the saddle.

Rico groans. "No, not more rules. What is it with city people and rules?"

Maxzyne rushes on, "Yes, but we can change the rules. See, it all starts with the alderman in my neighborhood. An alderman is a person elected by us. Well, actually, by grown-ups. Like my parents. Aldermen—or ladies—form the city council, which makes the laws, er, rules. But any citizen can give them an idea to make things better in the city." She snaps her fingers. "*That* person just has to take the new idea to the city council for a vote. And if they vote yes, the rule changes. That's how it works. Easy, huh?"

"Why do I think this is going to be harder than it sounds?" He yanks one of her braids and she ducks sideways to get free. "And who is your alderman person?"

"Alderman O'Malley. He spoke to our class last month. He'll be at the parade on Michigan Avenue tonight with the mayor and the whole city council."

"Hmm . . . and what do we change about the rule exactly? No more horses on city streets?" Caesar gives a high-pitched whinny, as if in agreement. Rico smiles and nods.

"Maybe," she answers, daring to let go of the saddle horn and wave one arm at the lake. "Or—I know! How about: Carriage horses can only be used along the lake or in the parks. So it's not so stressful for them to work on crowded streets every day. And the tourists still get a great view." She sweeps her arm again across the chilly moonlit landscape.

"Sí, I like this idea. This is a good rule for los caballos!" He leans around Maxzyne's shoulder, talking to Caesar. "What do you think of this rule, amigo?" Not getting an answer, Rico shrugs and makes a trilling noise with his tongue. The horse trots faster. "I think Caesar wants a warm barn and some dinner first," he tells Maxzyne. The horse snorts and his breath steams in the chilly air.

"First we've got to get to the parade kickoff on Michigan Avenue. All the city officials will be there. They have their own float." She admires the twinkling lights on the Navy Pier Ferris wheel getting closer. "We should turn soon 'cause Michigan Avenue and the parade starts that way."

Rico shifts direction, turning Caesar away from the lake. Within several blocks, the quiet desolation of the waterfront gives way to bustling taxis, cars, and buses. Rico keeps the horse close to the sidewalk, but as they near the parade route, the pavement is filled with pedestrians. Caesar whinnies, becoming skittish as a crowd of parents with excited children in tow swirl around him.

"The noise and crowds scare the horse too much," Rico frets. "This plan is no good."

"But we're so close. C'mon, chillax, Caesar," she coos while stroking the agitated horse's neck. "Let's pretend we're part of the parade and get close to where the city council hangs out. You can do it!" She pats him gently between the ears.

Caesar whinnies louder this time. The nervous horse dips his head, wanting to stop.

"C'mon, Caesar. We're almost there," Maxzyne urges. "Rico, do something. Can't you use that secret horse code to calm him down?"

"He is stressed. If he bolts, someone could get hurt. Better turn around before something bad happens."

"No," she snaps, pulling off her backpack and unzipping the canvas. "If you're not going to talk to him, I will." She fumbles inside and retrieves the black silk hat.

"What are you doing now, High-rise? That hat isn't going to calm him down."

Maxzyne tugs the hat down over her braids and resists the urge to jab Rico with her elbow. She is distracted when a small boy riding in a stroller points and shrieks, "Horsey, Mommy!" Rico skillfully guides the horse around the mother and child, but the sidewalk is crowded.

Maxzyne taps the hat brim. "This isn't just a hat, Rico. Don't laugh, but it's a magic hat. Caesar and I can understand each other when I wear it." She leans over and strokes the horse's neck. "Right, Caesar? So how can we help you calm down and get the city council to save you and all the other horses?"

"You are *loca*, High-rise. Maybe there is not enough oxygen where you live in that tall building. Your brain is starved for air if you think that's a magic hat," he scoffs.

"Be quiet and listen, Rico," she huffs. Rico shakes his head, pulling hard on the reins. Caesar stops. Frustrated, Maxzyne spins in the saddle. "Rico, what are you doing? I told you . . . Wait, look over there." She points over his shoulder. "We made it. This is exactly where we need to be." Rico twists the reins and turns to see a short, plump man wearing a red-and-green velvet bow tie. He is standing on a platform. Around him are several other official-looking men and women. Maxzyne cranes her neck, squinting at the blinking, battery-operated Santa face on the man's coat. The pulsing light reflects the familiar official's puffy cheeks and heavy jowls. The bags under his eyes are dark smudges.

"That's Alderman O'Malley!" she shouts. She flips one leg over the horse and slides from the saddle, dropping to the ground. Rico reaches to stop her but is too late.

Maxzyne pushes the hat away from her face and stands on her tiptoes, looking toward the officials gathered on a nearby platform. "I'll just . . ."

Alarmed, Rico stands in the stirrups as Caesar neighs and snorts, eyes rolling behind the leather blinkers. "Wait! Where are you going? I don't know how long I can hold on here."

Maxzyne points at the city officials. "Be cool, cowboy. Stay there; I'll be right back." She pretends to snap imaginary reins in her hands, flashing a grin. "I've got the reins on our city council. Just watch Team Maxzyne in action!"

She wades through the crowd, scampering around pedestrians. Several steps from the platform, she hears an angry shout from behind.

"Hey, there's Caesar! Kid, whadda'ya think you're doing with Mack's horse?"

9

Jerry the Balloon Man

*O*H NO! I'VE GOT TO GET BACK TO HELP *Rico and Caesar.* Maxzyne whirls around, braids flying from beneath the silk hat. She cranes her neck above the crowd, trying to see what's happening, but too many people push past her. *This is almost like when Officer Logan found me that time I was lost at Navy Pier five years ago. But I'm much taller now. Don't panic. Breathe.*

A young man wearing a Santa hat draped over his ponytail passes close on her left. That's when something pulls on her ankles, and she starts to lose her balance. Looking down, she sees that she has nearly been tripped by a dog's leash. "Hey, mister! Do you mind?" Annoyed, she bends down to unwind the leather strap from her feet.

"Dude! So sorry, man." He winds the leash tighter around his wrist, stooping to grin at his slobbering bulldog. Maxzyne turns away from the man and his dog, eyes searching for Rico and Caesar. *There they are.* She jumps up and down, arms waving, hoping to get his attention. *If he sees me, he could get Caesar over here, and we can make a getaway.* She tries standing on her tiptoes again for a quick glimpse. She sees a bearded man in a red silk scarf and porkpie hat stuffed over muttonchop sideburns. *Uh-oh. Looks like one of those carriage drivers. And now he's shouting at Rico.*

"I've got to get over there," she pleads, pointing as people swirl around her. But instead the crowd pulls her backward. She opens her mouth to scream. All at once, there is a familiar face in the sea of people around her: Jerry the Balloon Man. Surprisingly, the impatient pedestrians make way for his streaming rainbow of balloons, each artfully twisted into animal shapes, bouncing from a bamboo pole.

Jerry pushes an old bicycle with a ratty wicker basket. One glance shows it holds his balloon-making supplies. There is a scuffed air cylinder, ball of rubber bands, battered cigar box, bundles of string, and clear plastic bags of multicolored balloons. Maxzyne hasn't seen him since the weather turned cold and he abandoned his favorite spot on the corner of Randolph and Michigan Avenue. During the summer, his open cigar box was usually full of dollar bills from families with children visiting Millennium Park near her condo.

Over the years, she had collected quite a few of Jerry's airborne creations herself.

Instead of his usual threadbare T-shirt, the grizzled man wears denim overalls with a nubby green fleece jacket. He grins at her. "Hey there, Miss Maxie! What'cha doin' out here all by yer lonesome?" His gold front tooth flashes in the glare of a streetlight. Puzzled, he looks around for her parents.

"Uh, well, it's sort of a long story, Jerry. I'm trying to get back to somebody over there." She rises on her tiptoes, pointing. "See that horse and rider?" She gets a glimpse of Rico, still arguing with the stranger. "But it's so crowded right now." She leans against the bike's back tire, grateful to have an anchor for a moment.

"You got that right," he agrees. "I was tryin' to find a good spot on the curb where I could set up shop." He shakes the bike handlebars. "Got here too late, though." With a rueful shake of his head, he rubs his chin whiskers. "No place to work and still see the show, y'know? Can't do special orders for the kids till it calms down. Just hope I blew enough of these critters for the crowd tonight." He waves his bamboo pole, shaking the streamers of balloons.

Maxzyne gives a half smile. "I like your new penguin, Jerry." She points at the bird balloon near his shoulder. "But I don't have a place for it right now."

"Thanks, kiddo. Next time. Hop on and I'll get you over to your horse. Nice hat, by the way. You in the parade or somethin'?" He quickly stuffs the bamboo pole on the back of the bike. She hesitates, not sure what to do. He taps the cracked leather of the bike seat.

"Not if I'm standing here," she answers, swinging one leg over the bike seat. *That is technically true, right?* The muscles in back of her legs contract. *Owww!* Both legs ache and her backside burns from riding the horse earlier. It doesn't help that the bike seat is hard either. It feels a bit like the first week of soccer practice.

"Hold on tight, little lady. Let Jerry's magic balloons get ya where ya need to be."

Maxzyne grins and holds the worn handlebars with one hand and the hat brim with another. Her thoughts turn to her parents. *I'll need a magic balloon to get me out of the mess I'm in. And it will need to be bigger than the one that got Dorothy out of Oz.*

Jerry uses one hand to steer the bike as Maxzyne rests her feet on the pedals. Pedestrians let them pass. A little girl in pigtails trimmed with red and green gingham bows squeals, "Balloons, Mommy!" The tot points at the cloud of balloons overhead. "Not now, Susan," the annoyed parent responds.

Maxzyne cranes her neck, trying to see above the crowd. Her heart races, hoping Rico is still there. *First, I got him fired. Now he could be in trouble with the law. I'm supposed to be his "team" but everything I do makes it worse.*

The crowd thins as they leave the prime viewing area of the sidewalk along Michigan Avenue. Jerry's bike coasts through a group of standing policemen, all on the lookout for trouble on a busy night. Their radios crackle with official-sounding orders. She ducks her head and peers through her braids. Once they move past the policemen, her heart leaps when she spots Rico.

But it quickly sinks when she sees two men trying to take the reins from him. Rico is too quick, using his feet to keep them away. They shout, each trying to get control of the horse. *Is that the owner?* Poor Caesar neighs his displeasure. *He's really desperate to get away.* She has a flash of Lady Pearl consoling him in the stall earlier. "Caesar, hang on and we'll get you to a safe place, I promise," she pleads. The horse bucks, his eyes looking wild. Rico and the stranger fight over the reins as Caesar thrusts his proud head sideways. *He knows those guys and wants to escape.*

"Holy moly! What's goin' on here, Maxie?" Jerry's bike glides to a stop next to Caesar.

Maxzyne jumps off, holding on to the hat. "Those guys are mean to horses," she whispers breathlessly. "And we're here to rescue that one." She rushes over and pulls on the long, old-fashioned coattails of a carriage driver fighting Rico.

"Hey! Leave him alone," she yells. Distracted, the driver and another man turn around. A sudden gust of wind lifts Jerry's balloons, tugging at their strings.

Maxzyne grabs the silk hat's brim, keeping it from blowing away. Neon clouds of twisted rubber shapes swirl around the men, confusing them. Rico looks astonished to see her but takes the opportunity to shove the nearest man away with his pointed leather boot. Taking a firm grasp of the reins, he gives Caesar a quick tap on the left flank with his riding crop. Miraculously, the spooked horse responds to his signal to move to the left. Horse and rider start to turn back toward the empty side street in the direction they came.

"Rico! Caesar," Maxzyne screams. "Wait for me!"

10

Stop, Thief!

HEARING HER SCREAM, Caesar rises on his back legs, snorting. His front legs fight the air as he thrusts his head to look at her, dark mane streaming in the breeze. *I think he wants to rescue me.* All around, the crowd shrieks and claps. Maxzyne and Jerry can only watch in horror. "They must think this is all part of the parade or something," she worries. "Don't they know they could get hurt?"

"Look out," Rico shouts. *"Cuidado!"* (Careful!)

The two angry carriage drivers jump back and wave their fists at him. "We'll get you, kid! You can't steal a horse and get away with it!" With a final, desperate lunge, one man gets close enough kick Caesar in the lower hindquarter.

Rico is furious as he struggles to control the horse. Maxzyne gasps, feeling the white-hot rage of the horse as he veers sideways to protect his flank from the attacker. Suddenly, Jerry jumps between the two angry men and the departing horse and rider. Streamers of balloons bounce and float, making it difficult for the men to pass. The carriage drivers swat and bat at the balloons, looking comical in their antique clothes. Around them, the gawking crowd cheers.

"Thanks, Jerry." Feeling relieved that Rico and Caesar managed to escape, Maxzyne watches them trot in the opposite direction. "I'm stranded, but at least they escaped."

"Got a soft spot for the four-legged critters," Jerry admits. "You wanna follow?" He pushes the bike toward her. "You ride, and I'll drive, kiddo."

"Cool!" Maxzyne hops up to sit awkwardly in the handlebar basket, which is definitely *not* comfortable. Jerry pushes the bike down the sidewalk, through the crowd, and over the curb. "Make way, folks. Horse rescue here!" He gets a running start then jumps on, pedaling furiously after Rico and Caesar.

The crowd roars as they head down Michigan Avenue. Rico and Caesar are already two hundred yards ahead. Jerry's balloons stream behind them in the crisp night air, making a festive cloud of bouncing neon rubber. Onlookers lined up on the sidewalks spanning both sides of the wide avenue clap, wave, and point. A few children escape from their parents' grasp. Squealing, they try to follow the two on the worn bike, hoping to grab a balloon.

How awesome is this? It's just like being in the parade. Almost on cue, they ride past the city council's float. The hulking white three-level float is trimmed in red stars and sky-blue garlands to resemble the Chicago flag. Nearby, city officials line up to board the float where the parade platform sits at the intersection of Michigan Avenue and Delaware Place.

Maxzyne spots several majorettes practicing in sequined navy leotards and fitted jackets with white faux fur trim—her school colors. One by one, the girls turn to watch her pass. Astonished to see her, their twirling batons fall to the ground with a clatter. The tallest girl, a blonde with her hair coiled in a bun pinned with sparkling rhinestones, shrieks, "You're supposed to be suspended, Maxzyne!"

Courtney Crowder. She always has a way of making my day worse. Maxzyne's heart quakes at her classmate's shrill, smug accusation. But her super-annoying-on-steroids classmate is right. Maxzyne's in so much trouble now that only a miracle could save her. *Someday, I'll be old enough that I won't ever need to worry about being in trouble,* she vows to herself. *I'll be a grown-up and make my own rules.*

"Hey, Maxie," Jerry interrupts her daydream. "Check it out. We got our own little parade goin'. Half the police force is after us." He jerks his thumb backward. Holding the hat, she leans dangerously far from the handlebar basket to see. The bike wobbles and veers to the left. "Careful there," Jerry warns. "Just one driver here, y'know."

Shocked, she pulls her bouncing braids out of her eyes. Jerry is right. They've started a parade that spells trouble with a capital "T." Through the cloud of balloons, she can see horses and bicycles, all carrying uniformed Chicago policemen riding in their direction.

Breathless from working the pedals, Jerry pants while trying to talk. "Not runnin' from the law or somethin', are ya?" He takes a deep breath as his thin chest heaves under the nubby green fleece.

Maxzyne's mind races. How to answer? "Um, well, I'm not, er, actually *running*, right?" she calls back. *I am so busted.*

Jerry is panting so hard that he can't hear her. "I got nothin' to worry 'bout since my business license is right here in the cigar box," he reassures her. "Just hold on tight." Hunching over the handlebars, he pedals like a madman. Balloons trail in a rainbow cloud behind them. The crowd cheers and claps, everyone enjoying the spectacle.

Maxzyne can't look at him. "Uh . . . Jerry? I may be sort of running from the law." She swallows nervously. "Okay, I am. But just a little bit."

"Wh-aat?"

"I swear for donuts I don't mean to," she squeaks. Her explanation tumbles out as she clenches the handlebars behind her. "Rico and I went to see Officer Logan at the mounted police stables earlier." She doesn't dare turn to look at him.

"You got the law all riled up even before this chase? It's parade night. Are you crazy?" he wheezes.

"It all happened so fast. I didn't mean to. I, er, we just wanted to save Caesar. But when Officer Logan told us the horse was reported *stolen*—yikes! That's when we made our stage-left exit move. Okay, me. I freaked. It was my fault." *There, I've said it.* She takes a deep breath, her shoulders shaking. Just admitting her part in this drama to a grown-up makes her feel a tiny bit better.

Jerry nods, digesting her story. "Yeah, these cops are gonna want to blame somebody." His long legs continue to pump the pedals as he sneaks a quick look behind them. "Your folks won't be happy either, Miss M."

Maxzyne's stomach lurches, thinking about her parents. "Well, I was just trying to help a scared, lost horse. Plan B was to bring Caesar here so I can try to get the law changed for all the carriage horses."

"Huh? Change the law? Are you kidding? You're just a . . . Wait—how old are you?" he rasps, his voice rising.

"Eleven."

"Eleven? You're just a kid, kiddo. Think you're gonna change a law already on the books?" Jerry huffs and puffs, shaking his head. "Uh, not to discourage you, but do you even know what to do?"

"Yeah. I mean, I think so. We learned how it works in civics class. So why not try, right?" *Breathe.* She inhales, trying to keep her voice from shaking. "Anyway, I thought we could ask Alderman O'Malley for a vote to keep carriage horses off the city streets because it's so harmful to the horses." She cranes her neck, looking at the crowd of police closing in on them. *Uh-oh.* Her heart pounds.

Behind her, Jerry coasts on the pedals for a minute, wiping his red face on his shoulder. Picking up the pace again, he shouts, "But those carriage drivers will lose their jobs."

"No, they could still take tourists around. But stick to the parks and along the lake where it's less stressful for horses. More fresh air and green space. That's all. Swear for . . ."

"I know, I know—donuts," he finishes her sentence. "You kids 'n your crazy talk and ideas. These days, I thought everyone's nose was in their smartphones or videogames, not messin' with the law." He jerks his thumb at the commotion behind them.

Up ahead, a stream of police are closing the distance between Rico and Caesar. From behind their creaking bike, a familiar voice calls her name. It echoes eerily through a police megaphone, making her want to disappear inside the cigar box she's sitting on. "Maxzyne Merriweather!"

How did Officer Logan find me?

"Maxzyne! You get off that bike right now and stop this nonsense." The angry officer trots into view. Riding Ace, his regal horse, he swerves close and points the megaphone at Jerry. "Sir! You with the balloons. Stop right where you are. Be advised you are in violation of Regulation 23.9825. Failure to yield right-of-way on a parade route. And Regulation 86.0732. Harboring a fugitive of the law."

She gulps, trying to decide what to do. *Geez, how many rules are there, anyway? Millions?*

"Jerry? Uh, I think they mean business. You better let me off. Otherwise, Officer Logan will be *really* mad at you too."

Jerry hunches closer, still pedaling like crazy. "Okeydokey, kiddo. Hate to see you in trouble with the law when you're just bein' a good friend to that horse up there." Still pedaling, he wipes his face on his fleece again. "Wait a sec. How 'bout this? First, I'll let 'em all go."

"Let all what go?" She leans backward over the handlebars, trying to understand him. He points his thumb skyward, grinning. "You mean your balloons?"

"Yup. My flyin' critters. That'll distract 'em, all right. You can get away and join yer friend up there on that horse. Got this far, now might as well get that law changed." Jerry's smile widens. His face is red and beads of sweat trickle from his freckled forehead. "Whadda'ya say? You ready?"

Maxzyne gives him a solemn nod. *This isn't even Jerry's problem and he's helping me. And Rico and Caesar.* She feels her chest tighten as tears gather in the corner of her eyes. *I hope I don't get him in trouble too.* Her voice wobbles a bit, catching in her throat. "Thanks, Jerry. If I get out of this without going to jail, I'll help you blow up balloons anytime. Swear for ice cream."

"Just hand me that box cutter in the bottom of my basket there, will 'ya? Yeah, under there—that's it." Maxzyne wriggles a few inches over, balancing on one hip to sift through the basket's contents. In a corner she finds the smooth silver box cutter. Still pedaling, Jerry swings his arm back and retrieves the knotty loop of strings holding the airborne balloons.

Beside them and growing more impatient, Officer Logan bellows again, "Maxzyne Merriweather, stop this nonsense now. Did you hear me?"

She flinches, nearly dropping the box cutter. Ace's hooves pound the asphalt as his flanks brush perilously close to Jerry's bicycle. Behind the wooden sidewalk barriers, people point and cheer, thinking the chase is just a part of the parade. Fifteen yards in front of them, Rico turns to look. But seeing Officer Logan so close behind, he urges Caesar on with his riding crop and boots. *Breathe.* Her heart pounds. Rico and Caesar are just a horse length ahead. She wants to shout for him to keep riding straight back to Uruguay. *Better to save himself and the horse.* She bites the inside of her lip, drawing blood. *So much for Team Maxzyne. Or Plan Maxzyne. I didn't want it to be all about me.* Her conscience flicks back to the school classroom earlier. *But it always is, isn't it? If I had kept that drawing to myself, none of this would have happened.*

Jerry stands on the pedals. His tires squeal as he brings the bike to a shaky stop. The distance widens between them and Caesar. Rico glances over his shoulder again. She can tell he is nervous. She waves, motioning for him to go faster, but he looks unsure. *Go, Rico. Go.*

In the next moment, the bike patrol's flashing headlamps and Officer Logan's commands over the megaphone spook Caesar again. There is another roar from the crowd. She can see that it's all too much for the skittish horse. He rises on two hind legs, neighing in fright. Rico digs in his heels, defying gravity as he holds onto the reins and desperately tries to calm him. Caesar swings his head back and forth, eyes rolling, breath snorting. Seconds later, he turns and bolts straight toward the crowd.

Behind the barriers, people run, screaming and shouting, trying to get out of the way. Parents yank their children from the oncoming horse as a barrier is knocked over. Rico pulls hard on the reins and manages to swerve the panicked horse back into the street. The spectators are shocked, unsure whether it was just a prank act or almost a real disaster. One brave soul in a black knit cap over longer braids than hers stands in the street and records the scene on his cell phone. Maxzyne exhales. *Whew. Good save, cowboy.*

"You! Get back on the sidewalk now." Officer Logan's megaphone command makes the young man vault over the fallen barricade, cell phone in hand. The police dismount from their shiny two-wheeled vehicles.

Jerry rests the bike near the curb. "Okeydokey. Breeze is goin' in just the right direction. If you hurry, you can still catch 'em. Here goes Plan B." He hands her the thick knot of strings and she quickly cuts them. Jerry grins, his gold front tooth glinting in the glare of the streetlight. He nods to the patrol, winks, and whispers, "Good luck, kiddo." She throws the silver box cutter into the handlebar basket, not daring to look back.

The balloons swirl, escaping in the chilly air. For a few precious seconds, Maxzyne has just enough time to hide in the colorful mass. There is another squeal of rubber on asphalt when Jerry takes off in the opposite direction on his bike. In the confusion, she hears Officer Logan shout from the other side of a wall of drifting balloons, "I'll handle this. Bike patrol, I order you to stop that horse. Quick, before someone is hurt."

The uniformed patrolmen search for their bicycles amid the swelling rainbow of balloons. Bystanders, hoping to swipe one of the rubber creatures for their kids, dart in and out of the street, shouting and grabbing strings. Others race to pop them. All around them, children squeal. Officer Logan spots Jerry escaping through the throng. "Get back here! All the balloons in the world aren't going to save you, buddy. Do you hear me?"

Maxzyne doesn't have time to watch what happens next. She turns back to where she last saw Caesar and Rico, running and batting balloons out of her way. "Rico! I'm here, Rico." She runs faster, waving her arms through the balloons, desperately trying to reach him. At last, the neon cloud drifts higher, clearing the air around her. What she sees makes her heart sink.

So much for Plan B, she despairs. Ten yards ahead, the bike police surround Caesar and Rico. Caesar's head hangs low, and his breath mists the cold air around his long nose. One officer holds the reins, while another shouts orders. The rest surround the horse and rider, their helmet headlamps blazing.

Maxzyne's breath catches in her throat as she sees the terrible scene unfold in front of her. She can't bear to watch but must. She clamps a hand over her mouth to keep from shouting as Rico sits on the horse, his shoulders slumped. Seconds later, almost as if he knows she's watching, he straightens in the saddle. Around him, the police officers swarm and shout. Rico slowly raises his hands. Looking terribly alone, he is arrested in the middle of Michigan Avenue.

11

Plan C

HER CHEST ACHES, but it's as if some sort of survival instinct has kicked in. *Can't let Officer Logan catch me,* she thinks. *I've got to help Rico and Caesar.* Maxzyne races to the right side of Michigan Avenue. There is the smell of butter and a wafting mix of salt and sugar in the air. Seconds later, she ducks to hide under a portable popcorn machine on the sidewalk. Fortunately, the crowd is too busy to notice. All around her, people smile and reach high for the balloons that are slowly drifting away.

"Thith ith the beth parade ever," lisps a starry-eyed child. He grins at Maxzyne, his front tooth missing, as he waves a just-caught reindeer balloon. She gives him a half-smile before rising to stand on her tiptoes. It seems as if Officer Logan has forgotten about her. *So far the coast is clear. Now what?* She scoots forward, easing through the crowd until the mass of people becomes so thick she can't get through. Frustrated, she leans against a huge concrete planter filled with pine boughs, red holly berry branches, and fake snowflake ornaments. Her brain whirls as she decides what to do next.

"Okay, Plan B was a bomb. Time for Plan C. Think!" she chides herself. From the street, another round of cheering and clapping begins near the start of the parade route. Curious, she climbs onto the rim of the planter to see over the crowd. Her legs wobble until she finally gets her balance on the curved ledge. Her risky perch is worth it when a group of bagpipe players in plaid march into view, heading south. *It's the parade kickoff.*

Excitement ripples through the crowd as the band marches close. Maxzyne exhales and joins the cheering throng, waving as the men and women in high-necked green jackets, trimmed in gold braid and buttons, pass by in perfect formation. She admires their tall black fur hats, plaid kilts, and knee socks with matching plaid ribbons. They remind her of the holiday nutcracker beside their condo's fireplace during the holidays. Her grandparents brought it back from Europe when she was four years old.

She watches the players' cheeks puff as their fingers work the wind instruments. The cheerful melody soars. Around her, the crowd stomps their feet in time to the music. The knot between her shoulders loosens, and she begins to feel a bit more optimistic. With a graceful leap, she jumps down from the planter. The black silk hat topples to the sidewalk, so she stows it in her backpack for safekeeping.

"Yeah . . . like Dad says, 'Success is going from failure to failure without losing enthusiasm,'" she mumbles.

It's hard work pushing through the distracted crowd. She weaves in, out, and around people on the jam-packed sidewalk. Lights flash from cameras held in spectators' hands as the floats pass by. Several local television station trucks are also filming the parade. All around her, the crowd cheers and whistles for the Blackhawks hockey team, currently ranked number one. Directly behind the sports team's float, two stately gelding horses carry the regal mounted police officers. Their eyes scan the crowd. Not missing a thing, one of them makes brief eye contact with Maxzyne. Too late, she recognizes Officer Logan. He raises his hand, pointing straight at her. "That's her. Maxzyne is over there!"

Her heart pounds. As if on cue, she feels the tightness in her chest again. *Quick. Exit stage left.* She ducks behind a big man in a polar bear suit selling felt Santa hats. *That's what I need. A disguise.* She grabs one of the hats, stuffing her telltale braids inside. The bewildered man turns clumsily in his white-fur suit. "I'll pay you back—swear for cupcakes," she screeches before darting away.

She melts into the shadows of a hotel skyscraper. Even the uniformed doormen are distracted by the parade. She slinks by them, doing her best to stay close to the towering building. Nervous, she takes a quick glance backward but can't see whether the police are still trailing her. *Plan C, Plan C, Plan C,* she hums over and over. The coast seems clear. If she hurries, she might still be able to catch the city officials before their float joins the parade.

Before she can move, a bell chimes from the pale brick church on the corner. She shivers in the brisk night air. Using her fingers, she counts the somber beats. It's seven o'clock. Any second now, the mayor will pull the switch that lights the holiday decorations along Michigan Avenue.

She glances at the black sky and searches for the moon. There is just a smudge of light breaking through heavy clouds. It reminds her of Rico and his grandmother's embroidered scarf. Despite him not believing in magic, Maxzyne truly hopes the scarf has protective powers for him and the horse. The church bells now chime a familiar holiday hymn. She listens, trying in vain to see the moon. *I'd settle for just a star right now,* she frets.

The chimes fall silent, and she shivers in the chilly breeze. *I could really use some magic. Or a Christmas miracle. Pronto.*

12

Taking a Stand

NEARLY OUT OF BREATH, Maxzyne darts between kids and adults on the sidewalk. She runs, pushes, and occasionally shoves as if her life depends on it. *Well, someone's does, right? Rico and Caesar's.* Despite the rush, she tries to remember her manners. Somehow she manages to squeak out an occasional apology as she presses through the scrum of people.

"Excuse me! Sorry! Passing through, please! Ma'am. Sir? Excuse me!"

For once, being eleven years old actually helps. Thankfully, when the grown-ups turn and see a kid, they let her pass. When she finally reaches the curb, she gasps, hands on hips and bent over at the waist, trying to breathe. Her braids swing free and she realizes the Santa hat disguise is gone. Once she catches her breath and takes stock of her surroundings, she grins. *Mission accomplished.* She's now front and center, standing right next to the city council float.

She eyes the thick black velvet rope marking the space for "City Officials Only." From past parades, she knows exactly where the mayor will pull the switch for the holiday lights on Michigan Avenue. She edges closer until she is steps away from the wooden podium with the Cook County seal. Her heart thumps harder. She has to remind herself that she's there on official city business. *Hey, I'm a citizen with a petition. It can't hurt to ask, right? All these grown-ups in suits can make anything happen when they change a law. That's what the alderman said in class.*

Maxzyne rises to her tiptoes again. The mayor's graying head shines in the spotlight of several local TV news cameras. His red tie and matching pocket handkerchief contrast well with his white button-down shirt and navy overcoat in the glaring light. She suddenly feels nervous about being so close to the center of attention. Everything seems so . . . well, official. Especially the security detail guarding the four corners of velvet rope. They stand with shoulders squared and their hands clasped behind them. They certainly look like they mean business—especially the "mean" part. For the moment, nobody appears to notice her.

She turns her attention back to the short, slim man at the podium. Mayor Ramírez scans the crowd as his wire-rimmed glasses slide down his nose. There is a smattering of applause, and he gives the audience a strained smile. His speech about Chicago being a city of light makes Maxzyne wish he'd get on with the lighting part. Until she remembers why she's there: *Plan C, Plan C, Plan C.* Actually, she's surprised he hasn't thrown the switch on the festival lights yet.

Finally, the mayor motions for the man behind him to step forward. She recognizes Alderman O'Malley immediately. He is taller and pudgier than the mayor, and his blue eyes crinkle at the corners. Best of all, he wears a navy sweater-vest trimmed in white snowflakes under his open wool coat with a blinking battery-operated Santa pinned to the lapel.

The mayor and alderman shake hands, smiling warmly. Around her, the crowd surges restlessly on the sidewalk, clapping half-heartedly until he jokes that they better pull the light switch since "a lot of kids want to get back to their homework." Around her, all the school-age children boo.

Ugh. School. Her shoulders and resolve slump until several voices in the crowd shout, "Jobs for teachers. Save our schools and teachers!" Throughout the street, there is an uncomfortable silence. The mayor leans against the podium, his lips tight and brow furrowed. *Note to self: It must be hard to be a politician. Especially when folks don't like what you say or do.*

Ignoring the protestors, the mayor announces, "Well, I guess it's time to get this holiday started, folks. Are we ready for the Magnificent Mile holiday season to begin?" The crowd begins to whistle, stomp, and cheer.

Mayor Ramírez reaches for the oversized switch on the podium. *It's now or never. Time to step up and help make a difference.* Maxzyne grits her teeth. Before she can change her mind, she ducks under the black velvet rope, startling the security detail. The burly men spring into action. Scared but defiant, Maxzyne stands her ground. She jumps up and down, waving her arms and yelling, "Save our horses, Mr. Mayor. Save our carriage horses!"

The mayor stops to peer over the podium edge. He looks confused. "Er, what did she say? Something about horses?"

"Get on with the light show already," a man in the crowd complains.

"Yeah, we ain't got all night, Mayor," another shouts.

Maxzyne dances around to evade the security guards. "Sir, I said, 'save our carriage horses.' You know, the ones taking tourists around the city." She lunges to the left, avoiding capture, and squeaks, "It's bad for them."

Overhead, the television drones buzz, their cameras suddenly swerving to focus on her. The spotlights blaze, making her squint. She raises her hands, trying to shield them, but two security men each place a hand on her small shoulders. She tries to shrug them off, but their grips remain firm.

The mayor looks flustered and Maxzyne feels her resolve crumble. She quickly considers various soccer moves she might use to escape but changes her mind when the mayor throws his hands up in the air and waves at the camera, the festival lights forgotten. He shakes his head at the men holding Maxzyne. "Think of the publicity, gentlemen," he chides. "After all, she's just a child. I think I can handle this."

"Now, young lady, what's all this talk about carriage horses? And can I assume your parents put you up to this? If so, I'd like them to step forward now." He scans the crowd around her. When no adult steps forward, he looks puzzled.

A television news reporter edges closer to the velvet rope, extending her arm with microphone in hand. Mindful of the security men who have moved back to their corner positions, the woman leans into Maxzyne. She lets the microphone hover near the young girl's chin. "Uh, no sir, Mr. Mayor. My parents aren't here. At least, not yet, anyway. But I'm sure if they were here, they would also want the horses to be treated better, sir." Aware of the microphone, her words tumble faster. "So as a citizen of Ward 42, I'm here to make a petition to the city council," she declares.

The mayor looks stunned. He turns, looking at the city officials milling around behind him. They shrug. Several seem to enjoy the mayor's predicament.

"Let her speak," a voice yells from somewhere behind her.

"Yeah! It's about time you listened to *us* for a change," another shouts.

With a frown, the mayor taps his glasses on the edge of the wooden lectern. He clears his throat again and nods at Maxzyne. "Ahem. Young lady, what's your name?"

"Maxzyne, sir. Maxzyne Merriweather." From the corner of her eye, she sees another reporter sidle close. The TV reporter glares at the man holding a small notepad and pen. He ignores the woman and takes notes furiously.

"That' s Maxzyne with an x, z, and y, sir," she adds helpfully. Around her, the crowd titters. The newspaper reporter nods, correcting the spelling of her name.

Standing at the podium above them, the mayor looks annoyed. "And Miss Merriweather, may I ask how old you are?"

"I'm eleven, sir." She hesitates for a second but continues in a rush. "Alderman O'Malley came to my civics class and taught us all about how to change a law. I took lots of notes, and we had a mock vote and everything."

Around her, there is outright laughter as the grown-ups in the crowd enjoy her honest response. Mayor Ramírez's mouth opens and closes in surprise. He turns toward the group of city officials behind him and points at Alderman O'Malley. "You responsible for this?" he growls. "Care to explain what this is all about, or do I just wing it with our young constituent, Mr. O'Malley?"

The alderman steps forward. "Happy to explain, sir. I do some community service in the classrooms now and then. Empowering kids, you know. For when they're old enough to vote, that is. But I'm certainly not familiar with this young lady or aware of her petition about carriage horses." He shrugs helplessly and steps back into the group of waiting council members. His colleagues clap him on the back, enjoying his discomfort at being called out by the mayor.

Mayor Ramírez turns back to Maxzyne. "So what's the problem with the city carriage horses, Miss Merriweather? They've been a part of our city transportation for over a century." He smirks at his history reference. "Chicago was built on the backs of horses. On this very street there would have been hundreds, perhaps thousands of carts, buggies, wagons—you name it."

"Yes, sir, we learned that in history class. Also, Henry Bergh founded the American Society for the Prevention of Cruelty to Animals in 1866 due to the mistreatment of horses in American cities." The mayor looks surprised by her knowledge of the facts. She pauses to take a shaky breath, trying to keep her voice steady. "It's hard on them to be on the crowded city streets, Mr. Mayor." *Breathe.* "See, I know this horse; his name is— well, it doesn't matter. But he wasn't taken care of very well by his owner. Worse, he's not even a carriage horse. He's actually a very smart show horse that can do tricks and stuff. Like dance moves."

The mayor picks up his glasses, tapping them impatiently on the podium. Maxzyne senses that her chance to persuade the mayor or council is getting shorter. She talks faster. "But, besides him, my petition is for all the horses. Why not change the law so that they stay on the lakefront or in the parks? Being on busy city streets like Michigan Avenue is stressful for them unless they're trained, like the mounted police horses are. Caesar, he's just the one I know personally. He's been taking tourists around, but he gets spooked by the cars and the noise and— and, oh yeah, the pollution. His owner's overworking him because he has physical problems too. It's just not right to do that to a horse, sir. That's why I'm here. To change the law." she declares. "It's not safe and it's not right!"

There I did it. Don't know if anything will happen, but I tried. She hears a smattering of applause from the spectators around her. Maxzyne swallows nervously.

She turns to look as various people call out from the crowd.

"Yeah, she's right. Somebody ought to call the Humane Society," booms a male voice. "Rain or snow, you see them out here on the streets."

"Have a heart! Get 'em off the streets, Mayor," shouts another.

"Traffic's bad enough without bringing horses and carriages into the mix," a man yells from further away. "We've got buses, bikes, and emergency vehicles to contend with already. She's got my vote." The crowd starts to clap and cheer.

Beside her, the newspaperman writes furiously and then pauses to look at the mayor. "Uh, Mr. Mayor, sir? You'll recall we did that story six months ago about the poor treatment of carriage horses despite city regulations. After an investigation, it was determined the law needed changing. For public safety. And the horses, of course." He winks at Maxzyne.

The mayor turns and frowns at Alderman O'Malley, who looks uneasy. He nods at the mayor and steps forward when the mayor addresses him again. "It's your ward she's talking about, Alderman. Ward 42. Didn't you bring this to city council for a vote?"

"Er, no sir, not yet. The retail stores insist it's good for business. Even in the winter, tourists love the carriage rides. They can check out the other restaurants or shops along the way as they enjoy the pleasure of an old-fashioned horse-drawn carriage. It's win-win—at least for most constituents. Right?" He trails off, looking to his colleagues for approval. Most of them nod. The alderman puts his hands in his coat pockets. "Tourism. Retail. Photo ops of our fair city are just a few good reasons to keep the carriage rides downtown."

"That's right, Alderman. I'm a constituent and I say, keep the horses, get rid of the cars," someone suddenly yells. Everyone turns around, trying to see who made the remark. A man raises his silk top hat trimmed with holly berries around the brim.

"And get rid of the politicians drownin' us in regulations," the man beside him bellows. He also wears a hat, although his is more like a tweed cap. Around them, there is laughter and a smattering of applause.

The two men raise their fists in the air while one screams, "These city rules are killin' us small business owners." By now, everyone realizes the men are carriage drivers. There is a ripple of tension in the air. "And the horses *like* workin' the streets. They need their exercise. My horse even has an online fan page."

The other driver chimes in, "Besides, they don't like bein' cooped up in a stall all day, y'know. Are you gonna put us and them in the unemployment line, Mr. Mayor?"

The mayor scans the nearby newspaperman, the on-air reporter with her microphone, and all the hovering TV cameras. "Miss Maxzyne, we will be sure to discuss this very important topic at the next city council meeting. You have my word." He turns and points at the city officials. "Right, council?" The group of fourteen men and six women nod, everyone looking very serious.

The matter resolved, the mayor suddenly grins. He holds up the giant silver light switch. "But for now, let's get back to the holiday lights festival, shall we, folks?"

The children in the crowd shriek with delight, chanting, "Lights! Lights! Lights!"

Maxzyne quickly interrupts. "But, sir, I'll be at school when you have the next meeting." *Unless I'm suspended.* "Can't you just discuss it now?" She waves toward the crowd and the waiting city officials. "I mean, everyone's here, right? And these folks might want to help you decide what to do." Forcing her lips into a shaky grin, she pleads, "What's a few minutes when it means so much for a horse, Alderman O'Malley? I mean, all horses, sir," she corrects herself.

Annoyed, the mayor throws his hands up in the air. "Young lady, there is a formal process for these sorts of things. You can't just come up here and disrupt the parade everyone's been patiently waiting for and assume we city officials are just going to pass a new ordinance." He jerks his thumb at the city officials. "Alderman O'Malley will take your name and get back to your parents about the matter. Perhaps they can find time to attend the next city council meeting and report back to you. Alderman O'Malley?"

Maxzyne swallows hard, disappointment rising in her throat. The alderman strides toward her, his open coat flapping around his gray trousers. His snowflake vest and blinking Santa no longer look very festive.

"I've got it covered, Mr. Mayor." The alderman acknowledges Maxzyne with a thumbs-up wave of his hand.

"Let's not be too hasty, Mayor," someone shouts from her right. The blonde news reporter hands her microphone to a spectator, and it is passed through the throng. The frustrated voice continues, "This shouldn't become one of your back-room deals to be swept under the rug when the public's not looking, She asked a simple thing, and you give her the runaround. What kind of message does that send to the younger generation about city government?"

A woman adds her gentle voice to the mix, "We want to inspire our children to vote. Let kids know they can make a difference."

Someone else shouts into the microphone, "What're you trying to hide from the kid, anyway?" She could almost swear it sounded just like Jerry. She turns around, heart racing. *Uh-oh. That means . . .*

Sure enough, Officer Logan appears, riding Ace. The horse steps neatly through the crowd, onlookers giving way to the majestic animal and police officer. Several children squeal and beg to ride the horse but are quickly shushed. As the horse and rider draw near, Maxzyne's heart plummets.

Busted.

13

Compromise

MAXZYNE SCRUNCHES HER SHOULDERS and looks at the ground, hoping the officer won't notice her. She barely listens to the mayor address the policeman, too nervous to even peek through her braids.

"Yes, Officer?" the mayor can barely hide his annoyance at the interruption.

Officer Logan reins in Ace just a few yards from where Maxzyne stands by the velvet rope. The harness oil on the leather mingles with the scent of hay on the horse's warm breath that puffs her way. "Sir, I just wanted to make sure everything is okay over here. This young lady has caused a little too much excitement on Michigan Avenue already tonight." She bites her lip and looks up. Officer Logan gives her a hard stare from his high perch in the saddle. Maxzyne nods and shrugs half-heartedly.

The mayor turns around and holds his arms up in a gesture of helplessness. Behind him, the city officials mutter. Caught in the glare of such public scrutiny, the mayor is unsympathetic. "You heard your constituents, aldermen and women. They want to see what goes on at city hall—well, here goes."

A city council member steps forward. The breeze swirls the hem of her long, camel-colored coat and ruffles her short auburn hair. Maxzyne spots a red-starred Chicago flag pendant on her lapel. The woman frowns, looking determined as she strides toward the podium.

"Excuse me, sir, but we can't do this right now."

The mayor looks at her, one brow arching. "And why is that?"

"Because we have no way of making a record of this, er, special council meeting, sir."

The arched eyebrow comes down as the mayor rolls his eyes. "Better come up with a better reason than that, Councilwoman Perzinski."

On Maxzyne's left, the newspaper reporter raises his hand. "Mr. Mayor, glad to oblige." He waves his pen and small notebook in the air. "Tools of the trade right here."

The mayor nods at the newspaper reporter. "Thanks, Jim. I owe you one." He turns back to the lady in the long coat. "Councilwoman Perzinski, does this have your approval?"

"It's a bit out of the ordinary, as far as procedures go, but I suppose it will have to do."

"Then I call this meeting to order," declares the mayor. He raps the wooden lectern with his hand three times.

Councilwoman Perzinski nods. She motions the other nineteen city council members forward, calling out their names to the reporter. Maxzyne is impressed by her efficient manner and commanding voice. She finally acknowledges, "A quorum present, sir, so a vote can be taken."

The mayor nods and taps his glasses on the wooden lectern. "So now that the city council has been called to order, are there any . . ."

"Excuse me, Mr. Mayor, sir!" Maxzyne steps forward. The mayor looks annoyed.

"Yes? What is it now, Miss Merriweather? We'd like to expedite this process as quickly and professionally as possible." He nods in Councilwoman Perzinski's direction.

"Well, sir, aren't we supposed to say the Pledge of Allegiance first? "That's what they taught us in civics class. I mean, to have an official meeting for the record, right? The pledge comes next in the city council rules of order—just saying." She shrugs, her voice trailing off.

The mayor sighs. "Yes, yes. If you insist, we can say the Pledge of Allegiance. Is there a flag somewhere we can use?" He scans the skyline to no avail and then looks to the crowd. "Anybody?"

An Iraq war veteran steps forward, his brawny frame exuding strength under a half-zipped leather jacket decorated with army patches. He pulls a small American flag and a booklet from an inside pocket. "Got this! And a copy of the Constitution. Carry it on me wherever I go," he offers and riffles through the pages of the booklet.

"That will do," Mayor Ramírez snaps. He places his right hand over his heart. Following his lead, the city council members, Maxzyne, and the crowd do the same. Soon they are all chanting the familiar words. "I pledge allegiance to the flag of the United States of America, and to the republic for which it stands, one nation under God, indivisible, with liberty and justice for all."

The mayor drops his arm to his side. "Everyone good with that?" He looks directly at Maxzyne. She grins and nods.

"Very well. Let us continue. Ladies and gentlemen, Alderman O'Malley, Ward 42, is making a proposal regarding carriage horses in the city."

Alderman O'Malley turns to his fellow council members. "We've heard from several citizens already who would like to continue the use of horses on city streets. And others who would prefer they would be banned. Any additional comments for and against?"

"Yeah! Horses belong on a racetrack, not Michigan Avenue," someone yells.

"Hold on! Just a darn minute here!" The two carriage drivers shove their way to the front of the crowd, waving their arms. "Mr. Mayor, horses are our bread and butter. We don't need the ASPCA, PETA, or anyone else tellin' us how to treat 'em, either. We give 'em a fifteen-minute rest and water break every hour they're on the streets. We even put a diaper on 'em since a regulation made poop illegal."

The mayor and two committee aldermen can't help cracking smiles. The crowd chortles as the city officials press their lips together, trying to keep a serious tone to the proceedings.

"Sure. Diapers. Now *that's* something a horse might wanna complain about!" the frustrated carriage driver pipes up. Mayor Ramírez slumps against the podium and guffaws. All the officials relent, broad smiles creasing their faces as they join in the laughter.

Maxzyne is relieved to feel some of the tension drain from the air. Recalling her time with Rico and his instinct to always put the horse first, she quickly turns the issue back to the horse's health. To prove her point, she stomps her foot on the sidewalk. "You're sure that walking on pavement or concrete for twelve hours a day doesn't injure horses?" she insists. Her voice grows louder. "It must put a lot of stress on their bones." She looks at the mayor. His eyes slide uneasily away. "And hooves," she adds.

With a sigh, the mayor motions to a short, frizzy-haired councilwoman standing alone on the edge of the parade float. "Councilwoman Hanson?" She nods, stepping down from the platform, her black patent leather shoes reflecting the glare of the television lights. He continues speaking as she walks toward his podium. "You're head of the Committee of License and Consumer Protection. Did you recently pass an animal welfare vote for horses?"

The woman nervously clears her throat. "Oh, yes, Mr. Mayor. This amendment made sure the horse-drawn carriages did not operate during extreme weather. You know, cold, snow, or heat." She cocks her head, giving Maxzyne a kindly smile. "We are very concerned for the well-being of the horses, dear." She looks at the mayor. "All animals, really."

"Okay, but what about their feet, er, hooves on the asphalt?" Maxzyne persists.

"Well, it says that the horse's hooves must be shod and trimmed with rubber heel pads or open steel-tip shoes to prevent slipping." The woman takes a breath. "And it forbids the animal to be driven, overworked, overloaded, or kept in a cruel manner. We think that about covers it." She looks at her fellow aldermen and women, who nod gratefully.

Maxzyne chews the inside of her bottom lip and winces when she tastes blood. *That lady sure must have made good grades on tests when she was in school. Who could remember all that stuff?* She frowns, thinking of Caesar's worn hooves. "But how can you be sure?"

Sensing her frustration, the woman replies, "Anyone caught violating these regulations will be fined up to five thousand dollars for each offense. Plus the owner may lose the animal." The councilwoman pulls a blowing strand of curly hair from her face and looks at the mayor again. "The amendment also requires the horses be examined every three months by a veterinarian. Does that answer your question, dear?"

Maxzyne shrugs helplessly. Behind her, the two drivers slap their hands together.

The man with the holly berries on his hat is quick to retort. "Like I said, right?" He points his thumb at the councilwoman. "Like she said!" His friend nods briskly.

The other driver continues, "But thanks for spellin' it out for her, madam." He turns to address the crowd, his gruff voice growing louder. "We're not the bad guys here. We're law-abiding, tax-paying citizens. Just like the rest of you."

The other driver adds, "Sure. A lot more to the job, see, than just taking tourists 'round. We gotta look after the horse, but who's lookin' out for us? That's what I wanna know. Besides, we got a right to make a living on the city streets. Are you folks gonna take that away? Huh?" He points at a spectator. "You?" He turns to another. "What about you?"

There is an uncomfortable silence. *Geez, there really are two sides to every story. The drivers have a point. It's hard to decide, and I'm all for the horses. Why would anybody ever want to be a lawyer? Or alderman?* she wonders. *What if you make the wrong choice? You could have a bad rule.*

She looks over at the newspaper reporter scribbling in his notebook. He holds the pen cap in the corner of his mouth. The TV reporter arches her eyebrows, waiting for someone to say something. Maxzyne stands on her tiptoes, hoping to appear older and more confident than she feels. She leans toward the woman's microphone and says, "But nobody has to stop working. I just think horses should be off the streets. You know, stick to the lake and parks instead. There it's safe for everyone. It's more natural for the horse. It's beautiful too. Is that possible, Mr. Mayor? Council Lady?"

"Way cool idea! Have a little compassion, people," urges a female teen with spiky hair to Maxzyne's right.

"It'd be more humane, certainly," a kindly grandmother agrees. "We can keep the tradition and yet give our four-legged friends a better environment.

"Yeah, that's a win-win for everybody." Maxzyne recognizes Jerry's voice from the back. She feels a warm flash of gratitude for his support. There is a smattering of applause that slowly swells as the crowd approves the idea.

The taller carriage driver bristles. "You gotta be kiddin'. We already lost our best city spots when you changed where we could wait for customers last year. I must've lost thirty percent of my income 'cause folks couldn't find me or my carriage on Michigan Avenue anymore!"

His friend adds his own complaint. "Like we don't have enough to . . ."

Maxzyne breaks in, "Don't have enough time to care properly for Caesar, you mean? He's *your* horse, right?" *There. I said it.* She bites her lip, afraid of what else she might say. The carriage driver's face slowly turns a purple color. He points directly at her.

"Whadda ya know about Caesar, kid?" he growls. "He went missing this afternoon, and I reported him stolen!" He glares at her, his muttonchops and beard bristling.

She straightens her shoulders, jaw set. "Yes, that's because he ran away! He was so stressed and scared by all the loud city noises—like firetrucks and horns honking and cars cutting close. He did the only thing he could to be safe—run. That's why he ended up in front of my school, and my friend Rico and I . . ." Maxzyne stops, flustered. How much more should she say about Rico?

She looks at Officer Logan, but his gaze is stern. A lump forms in her throat. Somehow she manages to swallow her fear and continue. "So my friend Rico, he really knows horses. He's from Uruguay and he's a gaucho. Which is sort of a cowboy, but maybe even better. Horses are like family to him, and his culture believes the horse spirit and rider are the same. I saw it myself when he calmed Caesar down. He saved me 'cause I was sure I was going to die when the car horn scared him and he took off with me trapped in the carriage." She dares another look at Officer Logan. Maybe she's imagining it, but could his eyes have softened a little?

She takes a deep breath. *Here goes.* "And Officer Logan, he saw it too. He saw Caesar earlier when we went to see if he could help us." Her chin quivers with nervousness, the words catching in her throat. Her mouth is dry, but she swallows and continues. "He knows horses too. And he didn't think Caesar was getting enough to eat. He saw scars on his legs. I wouldn't be here now, except we got scared when we were told the horse was reported stolen. It was my fault. I panicked. But when Officer Logan found us, he saw the horse go crazy again. Caesar hates crowds. He would've run straight into them, except Rico held on to the reins and saved everybody." *Everyone but himself,* she worries.

"That's right! Saw it myself tonight, just a couple blocks from here." The crowd rustles, craning their necks to see who is talking. Again, Maxzyne recognizes Jerry's voice as she listens. "That horse was scared all right. He reared up so high I was sure he was gonna fly.

Couldn't think how anyone could get that horse back to earth again. But that youngster ridin' him, he was a real pro. Kept that horse from hurting anyone!" His voice turns accusing. "And it didn't help that the bike patrol had him surrounded like that."

Everyone looks at Officer Logan. He shifts in the saddle, looping the reins around his right hand. "Well, that's true enough. I did see the horse panic, and we nearly had a tragedy occur. But through no fault of our men, to be sure, Mayor."

He points at the two carriage drivers. "And I'm no veterinarian, but I can verify that the horse looked undernourished and had scars when he was brought to the municipal stables earlier. It's true that it takes an exceptional horse, one with the right disposition and training, to be able to work these city streets." He leans forward and pats Ace on the neck. "Like Ace here. Born, bred, and trained to be a patrol horse. That's why he's so calm. The horse she mentions named Caesar? Don't know where you found him, but if he's originally a show horse, he'd never be happy on the streets. That's a high-maintenance performance animal. A good carriage horse requires a much more placid personality."

The carriage driver remains silent, his lips a thin, tight line between rusty muttonchop sideburns.

The officer continues. "I'm guessing Caesar's a fairly recent purchase. And he doesn't have the tattoo identification required by ordinance. So you've already got yourself a hefty fine, I'd say. He's been impounded for the time being." Officer Logan raises his voice. He turns to look at the mayor and council members. "The way I see it, folks, is this: if there's a chance any horse working on the streets shouldn't be there, that's a good enough reason to vote for a change in the law, Mr. Mayor. Aldermen . . . and women." He tips his shiny blue riding helmet slightly in the direction of the city council.

Maxzyne exhales, suddenly realizing how much she's been holding her breath. Her lungs fill, but her hands are still shaking. Listening to Officer Logan's official account of Caesar's attempted rescue and impoundment reminds her of Rico. *Where was he now? He'd be pleased to hear the policeman's fair and positive take on the situation.* She clasps her hands behind her back, crossing her fingers. Better yet, maybe the police officer's words would carry some weight with the mayor and city council.

The tall carriage driver with the holly-trimmed top hat looks sheepishly at the mayor. "Mayor Ramírez? Maybe we could just back up a minute. You know, back to that amendment about keepin' the horses on the parks or lake trails?"

The mayor arches an eyebrow at the man. "So now you want to work *with* us, eh?"

"Yeah . . . I guess I'd vote for that, sir. A ride in the park's better than no ride at all."

Mayor Ramírez turns to the aldermen and women. He grins and gives them a thumbs-up, saying, "Young Miss Merriweather, a citizen of Ward 42, has presented her petition to amend the horse-drawn carriage routes, restricting them to the parks and lake trails. Alderman O'Malley, since she lives in your ward, will you consider this proposed resolution?

Alderman O'Malley steps forward, nodding vigorously. "Aye, sir."

The mayor waves his glasses at the others. "Is there a second? Councilwoman Hanson? Do you second the motion?"

The short lady with frizzy hair beams. "I second the proposed resolution." Her voice soars as she proclaims, "Whereas there shall be an amendment to the Municipal Code for Horse-Drawn Carriages to limit their use to park and lake trails."

Around her, there is a loud chorus of "aye" votes from the council members. Councilwoman Perzinski quickly steps forward, clapping her hands for order. "Roll call vote, please."

The council members are happy to step in line as she calls their names. Maxzyne can't help noticing that most of them take full advantage of the television cameras as they step forward, stating their name and vote. Finally, they heard: "No 'nay' votes, Alderman. The motion prevails."

Just like that. *Huh? Really? Wow!* She bounces on her toes, thrilled. *We did it, Rico! I can't believe it. Did we really just change a rule?* All around her there is a groundswell of clapping that grows into thunderous applause. The television cameras pan across the joyful crowd.

The newspaper reporter standing next to her stops scribbling for a moment. He spits the pen cap from his mouth into his hand so he can talk. "Free TV time for our city politicos," he smirks. "Only thing better than seeing their own face on TV without paying for it is actually winning an election. And this kind of press helps 'em win the next one." He scowls, waving his pen. "Nobody reads anymore, but if they did, my notes for tomorrow's *Tribune* newspaper are right here." He taps the pen on his slim spiral notebook peppered with scrawls. He flips through several pages then looks at her. "Maybe you'll be a reporter someday, young lady. Keep your interest in the world around you. Change things for the better by calling folks' attention to it, right?"

Maxzyne shakes her head so hard that several braids bounce into her eyes. "Not a chance, Mister! Grown-ups are impossible to deal with, don't always follow the rules, and take forever to change the rules they've already got." The newsman chuckles. "Got a point there, Miss Merriweather. Got a point."

Councilwoman Perzinski beams at the cameras and turns to the newspaper reporter, who nods at her. She announces, "If there are no other items of business to be considered, this meeting is concluded. I motion that we adjourn."

"Motion seconded," Alderman O'Malley exclaims. "Let's get on with the parade, shall we?"

If only Rico were here to see this. I'm just the "B Team" without him.

14

Whose Hat?

HOPING TO GET LOST IN THE CROWD, the two carriage drivers slink away. Maxzyne sees them, slides her backpack straps from her shoulders, and shouts. "Hey, wait a sec! I almost forgot to give this back to you." Both men turn, looking bewildered. They wait as she retrieves the shiny silk top hat, offering it to Caesar's owner. "I found this in the carriage. It's very special, so must be yours, right?"

The men look puzzled. She waves the hat at the burly driver until he finally snatches the tweed cap he is wearing and replaces it with the silk top hat. His lips stretch into an oily smirk when it becomes obvious the fine silk headpiece is too small to fit over his large forehead. He struggles to push it down over his protruding ears and thick shock of salt-and-pepper hair. Despite pulling with both hands, the silk hat will not fit. His broad face slowly turns red as his partner guffaws and points. "Who are you kidding, Fred? Drivin' the queen of England now? Or maybe Cinderella to the ball?"

Much as she dislikes the carriage driver for his treatment of Caesar, Maxzyne almost feels sorry for him. His smirk disappears, and he whips the black silk hat from his head, tossing it back at her. Caught by surprise, she stoops to catch it before it hits the ground. "It ain't my hat, kiddo," he growls. Throwing his friend a dark look, he turns on his heel.

His friend hurries after him, whining. "I was just jokin', y'know. Where's your sense of humor, huh?" The two quickly disappear in the crowd.

Maxzyne sighs with relief. She hugs the black silk hat to her chest as her heart pounds. She should have known he didn't own it. *There's no way anyone could wear this magic hat and treat horses badly.* She smoothes out the wrinkle on the crown and returns the headpiece to the safety of her backpack. She feels a pang of guilt over Rico and decides to save the hat for him. He deserves it.

A familiar face appears in the crowd. *Wait, is that…?* The same wide smile but dark, worried eyes under a shining cascade of brunette hair. Rosa!

Rico's twin sister edges past several people in the throng and stops next to Maxzyne. The young horsewoman in the black leather riding jacket tries to smile, but her eyes are anxious.

Maxzyne swallows nervously. "Rosa, how'd you find me?"

Rosa quickly interrupts. "Where is mi hermano, Maxzyne?" The two fall silent, realizing they can't both ask and answer at the same time.

Rosa answers first, tossing her hair over her slim shoulder. "It was easy," she explains, her voice neutral. She sweeps her arm above and around them. "Big screens, TV, shop windows. Everyone's watching. I just follow the cameras." She tries to keep her tone light, but her eyes flash with worry. "And I am here for my job. *Our* job," she corrects herself and fans a stack of glossy printed cards. "Is he here? We need to tell people about the show." Maxzyne recognizes some of the horses and costumed people from the Old Horse Theatre brochure. Her heart sinks. *What do I tell her about Rico?*

She hesitates and, angry at herself, her question comes in a breathless rush. "Rosa, is the show still on? After everything that's happened, I mean. It wasn't Rico's fault, you know. Just mine. He was only trying to help and probably saved my life when I was trapped in Caesar's carriage. If it wasn't for him . . ." She shivers in the frosty air. "I'm sorry. I really didn't mean to get anyone in trouble." Rosa remains silent. Maxzyne's voice shakes. "I guess Mr. Stryker's really mad too?"

Rosa nods slowly. "Sí, but the boss still needs us. Says he will see how tonight's show goes. Papá fixed the stall, but he and mi madre worry. *Ojala que* (I hope) we get a big audience to start the season . . ." her voice trails off and she looks around. "But where's Rico? Everyone talks about that horse, but I don't see my brother."

Maxzyne opens her mouth to give her the terrible news, but Alderman O'Malley interrupts them with an apologetic wave. Rosa takes a step back, unsure about being so near an important city official. For several seconds, Maxzyne and the alderman exchange awkward smiles, his long arm reaching to grip her small brown hand. As the two shake hands, cameras again buzz nearby, recording it all.

"Thank you for your petition, citizen Merriweather. The motion is granted. On behalf of the city council, we express appreciation to you and your friend, uh, er, Ricardo."

"Rico," she corrects him, with a pointed look at Rosa. "Rico Callea." Rosa's dark eyebrows rise like birds about to fly away. Alderman O'Malley nods, noting the correction. "Of course. Rico. Mr. Callea, the excellent horseman."

"Gaucho from Uruguay," she reminds him. She glances at Rosa again, giving her a reassuring smile. "You know, sir? We should call it Rico's Law."

"Yes, with his skill he certainly is a credit to his country. Uruguay, you say?" The tall man pumps her small hand faster. "Please express our thanks for his, er, to both of you. For your support and commitment to all city carriage horses."

Maxzyne drops the alderman's hand and grabs Rosa by the arm, pulling her forward. "This is Rico's sister, Rosa, sir. Rosa Callea. And you can thank Rico by helping get the word out about the show later tonight at the Old Horse Theatre. It's just a few EL stops from here. Right, Rosa?"

The stunned twin nods, her thick-lashed eyes wide. She hands the alderman a glossy card. "Sí, señor. Uh, my brother and I invite everyone to the show tonight. It's *The Nutcracker*."

"On horseback!" Maxzyne adds. "It's way cool. You should see how good they are with the horses. I mean, scary good!" She smiles at Rosa, who gratefully returns the smile.

Alderman O'Malley glances at the card. "Can do," he agrees. "No time like the present." He winks at both girls. "Let's do this while we have the press paying attention, right?"

The two girls nod, delighted.

He waves over the TV news reporter and whispers his request. They both watch the camera zoom in, and the politician waves Rosa's card at the crowd. "Folks, if our city council vote wasn't enough horse love for you, go check out Chicago's longest-running horse show. The season opener for this amazing spectacle is tonight. This Nutcracker is like nothing you've ever seen. Come one and all, you won't believe your eyes. Horses, daredevil riders, and holiday magic. Located in the historic theatre right in the heart of Old Town, kids are sure to love it!"

Taking advantage of the free publicity, Rosa and Maxzyne weave through the crowd, handing out cards and encouraging people to see the show.

The TV cameras focus again on Mayor Ramírez, who waves impatiently from the lectern. He holds the giant light switch aloft and the crowd murmurs and points in anticipation. His fingers grasp the glowing plastic switch as he prepares to launch the holiday light show. Maxzyne and Rosa stand near the edge of the crowd, clutching their remaining show cards. Nearby, several bystanders begin to chant. "Lights up! Lights up! Lights up!" Rosa and Maxzyne wave their cards in the air, joining in the cheer. Feet stomp and arms wave impatiently.

In the midst of such joy, Officer Logan suddenly looms over Maxzyne, his shadow filling her with dread. With a light pull of the bridle, he nudges Ace to stand next to her. She can feel the warmth of the horse's strong withers, and there is a faint smell of hay mingled with saddle soap on the chilly breeze. The officer leans forward, giving her a stern look. "No celebrating for you, young lady. You've got a date with the law."

Beside her, Rosa gasps. "No!"

"But can't I . . . I just wanted to . . ."

"No more procrastinating, miss. You need to account for your actions now."

Maxzyne turns and pulls Rosa by the wrist. "Yes, sir. I won't cause any more trouble. Just please let Rosa come with me. She's Rico's twin sister and she's worried 'cause he's supposed to be in tonight's show." With an apologetic glance, Maxzyne squeezes the scared girl's hand.

Officer Logan frowns and for a long moment considers her request. At last, he gives a curt nod. With a black-gloved hand, he motions to two patrolmen standing nearby.

Where did they come from? Worse, where are they taking us? To jail?

They pay no attention to Rico's twin. Instead, each officer grabs an elbow, expertly guiding Maxzyne along the sidewalk. Unable to see Rosa, she hopes the girl is following behind. Curious bystanders step sideways, allowing them to pass. Everyone whispers and several people point her way as the police walk her out of the crowd.

"Isn't that the girl who . . . ?"

"Yeah, she just got the vote for city carriage horses. That's her."

"It's such a nice thing she did for those horses."

"Who would think someone so young could accomplish that? Where are they taking her?"

Officer Logan ignores the chattering crowd as he calmly leads the way, riding high on Ace's muscular back. The crowd thins noticeably as the small group heads away from the center of action at the mayor's podium.

Maxzyne glances at the man to her left. The black-and-white checkered band around his hat brim reminds her of the mysterious hat in her bag. *Where is the magic when you really need it? If only it would whisk me away from here right now.*

As if on cue, an explosion of light dazzles and nearly blinds her. Cheers and whistles are heard from the balconies overlooking the street, and there is a dull roar from the crowd a block away as the holiday lights turn Michigan Avenue into a winter wonderland of enchanting sparkle. Bare tree branches along the wide street twinkle, church bells chime, and children jump, clap, and shriek joyfully. She would join them except for her pinned elbows.

Despite the display of holiday spirit, the two officers shuffle her forward on the pavement. Her gaze returns to Officer Logan. His regal horse steps carefully, and the merry city noises drown out the sound of hooves on the sidewalk. Maxzyne can only look at Ace's graceful, flowing tail as he patiently leads the way. She ducks her head, unable to wipe away the two tears sliding down her cheeks as she is marched toward the police parade headquarters.

15

Command Center

MAXZYNE SWIPES UNDER HER EYES as soon as the police officers let go of her elbows and guide her through a blue plastic flap. From what she can tell, it seems to be the entrance to a temporary structure built just for the parade. Another officer in uniform sits at a computer, monitoring the crowds on Michigan Avenue. There is the occasional crackle of static over the police radio channels, making it clear that this is an official command center tucked away on a quiet corner two blocks from the main route of the parade tonight. Normally she'd be very curious, but right now she is too nervous about her future. *First the principal's office and now the police. How do I always manage to get myself in trouble? And that doesn't even count the trouble I'm in with my parents.* Her stomach lurches and gurgles in fear and hunger.

From behind, Rosa squeezes her on the shoulder. Maxzyne turns and looks gratefully at Rico's pretty twin sister. More guilt swirls in her gut. This was all her doing. Now she can only hope the police will be fair to the Callea family in spite of all the trouble she has caused everyone.

Seated nearby, a uniformed dispatcher with a laptop listens to coordinates of potential trouble spots called in by roaming police officers. *This must be how Officer Logan found me. Eyes and ears everywhere.* Maxzyne looks warily at the two police officers who brought her here. They ignore her, talking softly in the corner.

She turns to look at Rosa, who shakes her head and shrugs. "Where'd Officer Logan go?" Maxzyne whispers. "Maybe he's getting Rico now," she offers hopefully.

Rosa nervously weaves her fingers through the thick waves of dark hair. "I told mi hermano not to do anything stupid." Her eyes flash for a second. "That horse didn't belong at Stryker's." Maxzyne looks away. As if reading her mind, Rosa continues, her voice growing softer. "Even if you were trying to *ayudar al pobre caballo* (help the poor horse), Maxzyne, it didn't help *us*."

"Will you lose your jobs now? Your home in Uruguay because of me?" Maxzyne's voice cracks. "I mean, Mr. Stryker didn't seem very nice, and now I'm afraid . . ."

Rosa looks thoughtful. "Sí, Mr. Stryker is a tough guy. A boss who means business." She waves the glossy cards in her hand. "But he does know show business. Maybe he thinks about the money a little too much. And my gaucho brother thinks of the horses a little too much. Right now, we all need each other." She shrugs, smiles faintly, and flips her hair back over her shoulder. "Mr. Stryker gives us our show business break here in the city. We can ride the horses and make money too. My hope is to someday have our own show."

"But don't you want to go home to Uruguay? Ride on the plains again? That's what Rico said he wants."

Rosa chuckles and shakes her head. "No, not me. I love the show. It is *emocionante!*" She waves her arms skyward.

Maxzyne is confused. "Emocionante? Like emotional?"

"Umm . . . no . . . How do you say it? Exciting. I ride high on the back of a horse, wear a beautiful costume, and find new ways to entertain the people. It is all exciting." She looks around, suddenly frowning. "I think for my brother it is exciting too. If he would give this new life a chance. *¿Pero dónde está Rico? Me estoyempezando a preocupar.*" (But where is Rico? I'm getting worried.)

Maxzyne doesn't exactly understand what Rosa just said, but she can pretty much guess by the worried look on her face. "I know. I'm sorry, Rosa. If only . . ." She sighs. If only she had a pencil right now. She'd draw something else and take her mind off her problems. Better yet, draw something for Rico. It was the least she could do. She looks around the room and spots a notebook and several pens on the table beside the seated policeman. "Excuse me. Uh, sir? Do you mind if I use one of these pens?" Her voice squeaks a little, embarrassing her.

The man doesn't even look up from the computer screen. "Sure, kid. But no funny business. Captain Logan will have our heads if we lose you again. He's taken a personal interest in this case, so no trouble."

"No, sir. Not me." She grabs a blue ballpoint pen from the table. Rosa watches curiously as she retrieves the doomed sketch of Miss Garrett from her pants pocket. She carefully unfolds the page and turns it over. Seconds later, she forgets everything except the drawing of a horse and young rider that takes shape under her skillful eyes and fingers.

Rosa gasps and points at the figure seated on the horse. "Sí, I know this one: mi hermano, Rico, and that horse."

Maxzyne nods, filling in the details. She adds Rico's bandana, Caesar's bridle, and several bold slashes to enhance his mane and tail. As an afterthought, she adds a background of hazy clouds and a full moon rising over a gently rolling lake.

Rosa whistles low between her teeth. "You are good. *Buena artista* (a good artist)."

Maxzyne grins as Rosa admires the sketch and gives her a nod of approval. "Thanks, Rosa."

It means a lot to hear such a compliment coming from a talented and pretty girl like Rosa. Maxzyne scrawls her signature across the bottom of the creased page, trying to explain. "My drawing got me into a lot of trouble today at school." She swallows hard before continuing. "Sometimes I think it's the best and worst part of me." She blows on the ink and touches the page with her index finger, squinting at it. "But because of my mistake in class, I saw the horse outside and then I met your brother. Will you give this to him for me? Rico should have it. I never met a gaucho before, and he saved the city carriage horses today. Really, it was all him, Rosa."

She looks up just in time to see a shadow cross Rosa's face. Maxzyne quickly tries to reassure her. "I mean, you can take it now, just in case he's already back at the show barn." She offers the drawing to the girl, waiting.

Suddenly, there is a swirl of voices outside. Her stomach shrinks and twists into knots when she recognizes her mother's anxious tone. "Where is she, Officer? Please tell me she's all right after this . . . this misadventure!"

16

Officer Logan's Discovery

"CALM DOWN, JERI," her father's soothing, unshakable voice responds from right outside the temporary enclosure.

How many times has he had to be the one to keep our family steady? Maxzyne sighs to herself. Her pretzel-twisting stomach nudges into her throat. *All because of my misadventures.*

The plastic flap is thrown back, and the two officers in the corner stop talking. They quickly move to stand beside Maxzyne. All eyes are on the entrance as everyone waits. "Right this way, folks."

Officer Logan's brisk voice of authority makes Maxzyne's stomach jump. *Breathe.* She reaches behind her and clutches Rosa's hand. "My parents are here," she whispers.

Officer Logan enters the temporary structure, looking small without Ace. He holds the plastic flap aside and waits as Maxzyne's mother enters. Her dark brows arch, brown eyes flashing wide, once she recognizes her daughter.

"Maxzyne! Are you all right?" The tall, elegant woman's face flushes pink under her dusky complexion. She rushes to hug her daughter, the familiar smell of cappuccino and her favorite perfume wafting in a cloud around her. Maxzyne's bottom lip quivers, but she manages to remain cool. The warm hug and fragrance comfort her as she peeks over her mother's shoulder at her father. She sees her school books in a clear plastic bag casually slung over his shoulder.

"Dad, you found my books?" her shaking voice squeaks.

Behind her father, another man emerges from the plastic-draped entrance. She recognizes his brusque, growling speech immediately. "Believe you left 'em in our stable, young lady." Mr. Stryker jerks his thumb at her parents. "Good thing. Only way I knew who to call." The beefy man adjusts his flannel cap over his forehead.

Her father looks amused. "We knew you wouldn't want to miss any homework, kiddo." He turns to wink at Officer Logan. "Heard you might have a lot of time on your hands after this latest escapade of yours." He leans toward her and lowers his voice dramatically. "Jail time."

Her mother whirls around and glares at her husband. "Max, don't say that even in teasing. She'll have plenty of punishment, but jail? That's a little ridiculous. She's only eleven years old."

Maxzyne desperately wants to change the subject. She quickly thrusts Rosa forward. "Mom, Dad, this is Rosa. She's a super-cool, amazing rider at the Old Horse Theatre by my school." She glances at Mr. Stryker, who nods. "And this is her boss, Mr. Stryker. He's in charge of the show."

The introductions give her a chance to stall any talk of future punishment. "They're having a show tonight and I, uh, saw the rehearsal. It's so awesome! Alderman O'Malley announced it on TV tonight. You should see what they do with *The Nutcracker*, 'cause Rosa and her brother, Rico, do this trick where they . . ."

"That's enough tricks from you for one night, Miss M. I think Officer Logan has something he'd like to say to you." Her father motions to the policeman. The officer clears his throat, looking stern. "Young lady, you caused a lot of chaos out there tonight. It ended well, but someone could just as easily have been hurt. I had to use a dozen of my men to chase you and that unstable horse down. And we all know they should have been monitoring and managing the parade crowd instead." He pauses, letting his lecture sink in.

Maxzyne clasps both hands behind her back and looks at her shoes. She nods, her braids falling over her face. She can feel her cheeks burn as she tries to keep from saying anything that might get her in more trouble.

Her mother reaches down and pulls her daughter's chin up. "Look at the officer when he's talking, Maxzyne. I don't understand how all this happened. We've always taught you to respect authority. Haven't we?"

Maxzyne nods again, focusing on the policeman. Her voice quavers. "Yes, ma'am." She swallows. "Yes, sir."

Officer Logan kneels down to crouch at her level, letting one navy-clad knee rest on the floor. "Maybe the most important thing is something that you aren't thinking of right now." His earnest face is inches from hers as his voice goes soft. "*You* could have been badly hurt." He leans backward, glances at her parents, and ticks off his concerns on one gloved hand.

"First, at the police stables you were not wearing a helmet as you rode that stressed, powerful horse."

Maxzyne's mother gasps, both hands flying to her cheeks. "Tell me you didn't, Maxzyne." Her daughter hangs her head, nodding.

Officer Logan continues. "And then we had to chase you and the balloon man down Michigan Avenue on his rickety old bike, didn't we?" Maxzyne nods again. "You put yourself in a lot of danger, missy. Do you realize that?" His blue eyes flash with concern.

She swallows hard, a lump in her throat. Her voice cracks. "Yes, sir. I know."

The policeman takes off his hat, letting it rest on his knee. "I would never want to have to visit you at the hospital, Maxzyne. My job is to protect people. And that means looking out for *all* of the people out there celebrating in our city tonight." He points at the oversized screens displaying the parade route before turning back to her. His voice hardens. "That horse had no business being on the streets."

Several feet away, Mr. Stryker growls under his breath. "Better believe it. That horse messed up my stall real good." He gives Maxzyne's father a pointed look. "Scared my show horses too."

Officer Logan ignores him, instead shaking a finger at Maxzyne. "Having said that, you were right about Caesar. If it weren't for that young man's ability to control that nervous horse, he would've broken through the crowd. He really could have hurt a lot of people. Instead of a parade, there might have been ambulances."

Rosa leaps forward. "Rico stopped the horse? ¡Mi hermano! Sir, have you seen my brother? Where is he now? Is he okay?"

Officer Logan rises, using his hat to dust off his navy pants at the knees. Finished, he carefully centers the brim of his hat on his forehead. He turns toward Rosa. "You say that young man is your brother?"

She nods solemnly. "Sí, señor. Is he here? Can I please talk to him?" Her voice turns plaintive. "He does not mean to cause any trouble. It is only his love for the horses."

The policeman gives her a curt nod. "Yes, I believe you are right. He didn't mean to make a getaway necessarily." He turns back to Maxzyne, one eyebrow raised. "I believe that was *you*."

She cringes, afraid to look at her father. "Yes, sir. It was me."

The officer points at Mr. Stryker. "And I believe the young man works for you at the Old Horse Theatre?"

Mr. Stryker nervously licks his lips. "Yes, he's part of the show, Officer." He jerks his large head in Rosa's direction. "Her too. The whole family helps with the show." He crosses both arms across his chest, squaring his shoulders as if expecting the worst.

"Well, you should know that after a brief investigation of the situation, he has been released from police custody," Officer Logan responds.

Rosa hugs Maxzyne, thrilled with this news. "Oh, gracias! Thank you, sir. Can I see him?" She joyfully jumps from one foot to another, forgetting her usual composure.

Mr. Stryker looks at his watch and mutters under his breath. "Good. Showtime's in ninety minutes." He motions to Rosa. "C'mon. The phone's been ringin' like crazy. We got an audience tonight thanks to all this horse drama on the TV news. Let's go!"

Officer Logan puts his hand on Rosa's shoulder, stopping her. "Not so fast, Mr. Stryker. According to my patrol's investigation, these young people are working without official state employment certificates." He turns to Rosa. "How old are you, young lady?"

Maxzyne's heart plummets as she recalls Rico's distrust of police and government officials. Her eyes squeeze shut as she imagines getting the twins in trouble. *Oh no. This is all my fault.*

17

The Dreaded Sketch

ROSA'S VOICE TREMBLES. "Thirteen, sir. My brother Rico is thirteen too. We are twins."

Mr. Stryker jumps in. "That's right, Officer. And they have their parent's permission to help out with the show." He glances at Maxzyne's notebooks. "That is, of course, when they're not at school."

Rosa clenches her hands, afraid to speak. Beside her, Mr. Stryker crosses his arms over his burly chest and smirks.

Officer Logan rests a hand on Rosa's shoulder. He looks squarely at Mr. Stryker. "So after you pay the outstanding fines for not registering your young employees, you'll get the required forms signed and submitted to the State of Illinois as soon as possible, right?"

Mr. Stryker's lips turn downward. "Oh yeah. We're a little behind on the paperwork lately. Sorry 'bout that.

Hey, any chance you can give us a break on the fines—just until tomorrow? You know, call this a grace period or something?"

"That's up to the mayor and the state. But I am curious what you're having them do at the Old Horse Theatre. The rules are clear; kids this age are restricted to very few jobs."

Mr. Stryker gives a nervous laugh. "We don't want any trouble with child labor laws." He twists his cloth hat in his hands. "Truth is, uh, these kids are kind of a special situation. They help with the horses, so that's like farm work. And riding in the show, well, that's just like child actors, right? So they're in two categories. Both legal, last I checked." He slaps his hat back over his bristly hair as the policeman stares down the theatre owner's defiance. After several long seconds of silence, Mr. Stryker's gravelly voice softens as he backtracks. "All kids these days have activities before and after school, Officer. Horses are their thing, that's all. And they're good at it. Right, Rosa?" He looks to the scared young girl for confirmation.

"Sí," she whispers. "We are gauchos." She looks at Stryker and chooses her words carefully. "We want to be with the horses."

Officer Logan taps the badge on his chest. "And we want to be sure all the rules are being followed for our kids." He turns to Maxzyne, eyebrows raised. "*All* kids.

Even when they're trying to save the world—the horse world, that is."

There is a small chuckle from her father. Maxzyne turns to see him wink in her direction, before her mother gives him a sharp look. *Maybe I won't be in lockdown for the rest of my life,* she tries to reassure herself. *At least Dad might go easy on me.*

Officer Logan nods at Rosa. "My men will be following up with school officials to be sure that *everyone* has time for their studies."

"Sí, er, yes, sir," Rosa whispers. With a nervous hand, she pushes her hair back behind one ear and then the other.

The policeman's voice hardens as he looks at Mr. Stryker. "And you can be sure that the proper tax authorities will be notified so that all employees are paid an appropriate amount and taxes are recorded."

"Got it. Yeah, will do," Mr. Stryker stammers. The theatre owner turns to glare at Maxzyne. "Thanks a lot, kid. This is all your fault, y'know. Never would've happened if you had just minded your own biz and left us out of your drama today."

Maxzyne wishes she could hide behind her father, but she knows better. Instead she squares her shoulders and looks directly at the theatre owner. "Yes, sir. Me too. I'm sorry I caused so much trouble to everyone. And if I don't go to jail . . ." Her eyes flick toward Officer Logan and back to Mr. Stryker. "Then maybe there's something I can do to make it up to you. I, uh, I don't know much about horses, but I can learn." The burly man looks skeptical. "Really. I can help feed them, clean them—anything. Oh, and I can draw too. I mean, in case you need some posters for the show or something . . ." Her voice trails off.

Rosa reaches into her jacket and pulls out the drawing of Rico and Caesar. She unfolds the page and shows Mr. Stryker the sketch.

"¡Sí! She is very good, sir. Look, she did this for Rico."

All eyes are on the drawing as Mr. Stryker reaches for it. Frowning, he gazes at the bold lines of the horse trotting on the lakeside path. He strokes the stubble on his bristly cheeks with his free hand, thinking out loud. "Hmm. Not bad. You say you can do more like this?"

Maxzyne nods vigorously. Mr. Stryker jabs his index finger at the page. "But instead of this lake background, maybe switch it up. Make it my theater. Yeah, with the performers in costume. And in color." He grows more excited. "Well, why not? We can use some good artwork." He nods at her. "It's a deal, kid."

Her mother reaches out and takes the sketch from his pudgy hand. "Actually, her name is Maxzyne," she reminds him. "And she did take responsibility for her actions, which was *very* grown-up of her." Her eyebrows arch as she gives the Old Horse Theatre owner a pointed look.

Wow. She's sticking up for me. Maxzyne's heart flutters with hope for a moment. It quickly fades when her mother turns the sketch over. *Uh-oh.* The one sketch she's not proud of drawing. She is so worried that she barely notices when Officer Logan motions to Mr. Stryker. The two step away from the group and then exit the command center.

Her mother takes one look and shakes her head. "This is the sketch of your music teacher? The one that Principal Farwell told us about, right?"

Maxzyne's heart plummets. She gasps, her voice catching in her throat. "You talked to him already?"

18

Getting in Harmony

HER MOTHER'S FROWN EXPANDS to that spot between her eyebrows. "Yes, I did. By sixth period, the school called me. Apparently, you were nowhere to be found. I couldn't believe you were sent to the principal's office for disrupting music class and disrespecting the teacher with this . . ." She throws her hands up, exasperated. "And I don't need to tell you that you are in *big* trouble." She waves the sketch of Miss Garret and her stubbly legs. "Before you try to squirm out of this, the school staff will expect an apology and who knows what else, Maxzyne. This is the kind of stunt that gets students kicked out of school."

"B-but, I can explain. That, uh, that sketch isn't totally my fault," she squeaks. "I mean, I drew the initial picture of Miss Garrett, true. But other kids in the class made those additions. I swear for cupcakes, Mom."

"There is no swearing for anything in our house, young lady. Max, you better handle this." She looks at her husband and fans her face with the sketch. "I'm so disappointed in her actions today."

Her father takes the sketch from her mother's slim brown hands and carefully folds it along the creases. Worse, he says nothing. Maxzyne can sense his disappointment by the way his shoulders drop and sag forward. His disapproval makes her feel worse than anything in the world. *I only ever want him to be proud of me,* she thinks.

With a sad look, he hands the sketch back to her. "We can't have you disrupting class, Maxzyne. It's not fair to the other students or the teacher. This time the punishment will have to fit the crime."

She wants to cry but doesn't dare. It would be worse to be a crybaby. "Yes, sir. I will do whatever the school wants."

Officer Logan suddenly reappears with Mr. Stryker. Behind him, Rico's mischievous face appears, framed by waves of dark hair. He flashes his signature smile.

Rosa darts forward, throwing her arms around him. "Rico! You are okay. I was so worried for you, little brother."

Her twin frowns. "What do you mean *little*? Just a few seconds, is all." He points his thumb at his chest. "And I'm taller than you." Rico straightens his shoulders and grins at her. Rosa just laughs and ruffles his hair.

Maxzyne leans forward to squeeze his forearm. She can't quite muster a smile but is terribly relieved to see him. *Where's Caesar?* she frets. She swings the backpack strap to her other shoulder and feels better knowing that the silk top hat is safe inside.

A keen observer, Officer Logan glances at her parents' faces, noting the tension. Seconds later, he takes the silver whistle from his pocket and gives it a quick, soft blow with his lips. This gets everyone's attention.

"I have an idea," he announces gruffly. "Before we lock Maxzyne up and throw away the key, maybe we should explore our options. Given that she and Rico have actually done a bit of community service today for the carriage horses, perhaps we can be more lenient." He pauses as her parents look skeptical.

"Despite all the trouble she's caused tonight?" her mother asks. "I can't imagine."

"We're listening," her father quickly adds. He gives Maxzyne a reassuring nod.

The officer shrugs. "Due to the positive outcome, maybe we can consider that time served," he proposes. He turns to point at her. "Of course, I expect that your 'community service' will continue," he urges her. "Unless you'd rather give Ace's stall a good cleaning for the next few Saturdays." He winks at Maxzyne's father, who gives an approving chuckle. Beside him, her mother shudders.

Rico beams. "¡Sí! Gaucha, you can learn about horses from the ground up."

Maxzyne wrinkles her nose, trying to be brave. "No problem, Officer Logan. A little stinky horse poop won't hurt me."

The officer grins and points at the sketch in Mr. Stryker's hand. "Actually, your skills with pen and paper might be more useful. The Chicago policeman's annual fundraiser is coming up soon and we could sure use your help designing the invitations. What do you say?"

"You can count on it." She beams. "Thanks, Officer Logan." She turns to her father. "But what about Principal Farwell? Am I still going to be suspended?"

Her father clears his throat. "Actually, I think we persuaded him that you could be more useful *at* school."

Maxzyne's mouth falls open in surprise. "You did?" She glances at her mother and quickly remembers her manners. "I mean, Dad, that's awesome. How?"

Her father glances at her mother before speaking. "Well, it's only right that you help the person you most hurt, Maxzyne."

"You mean Miss Garrett," she groans.

"That's right. And the principal says she has a terrible time keeping you and your classmates in line during class and thinks she might stop teaching altogether next year."

"That's so sad," Maxzyne whispers. "I feel terrible. I never meant to change her mind about being a teacher. I was just trying to get through my worst class at school." She turns to Rico and Rosa, rolls her eyes, and makes a face. "Really—folk tunes!"

The twins look mystified. "You don't like to sing?" Rosa asks.

"Not folk music. That's why I was doodling. Once my sketch went viral in the classroom and upset Miss Garrett, I was pretty mad." She squares her shoulders and gives Officer Logan a determined look. "At everyone but me."

Officer Logan's eyes twinkle as he taps his badge. "Yep. I see it all the time. Ace and I, we cuff a lot of folks who have that same feeling. Blame everyone but themselves. All the way to jail and the judge."

"Yeah. I didn't think it was my fault then," Maxzyne agrees. "But as much as I hate having rules, today I learned that we need them. Rules in school, rules for horses, rules for people. Otherwise, things get crazy." Her voice drops. "Dangerous, even." She turns back to her father. "So how can I help Miss Garrett?

Her father grins. "Well, like I always say, Maxie, 'I do my best work when I'm in harmony with the stock market.' I guess you'll be speaking to Miss Garrett about how you can be in harmony with her in the classroom."

"Maybe there is other music you can show her, Maxzyne," Rosa offers. "Me? I love classical guitar from Uruguay."

Rico scoffs. "No, my favorite band from Montevideo is *Buenos Muchachos* (Good Fellas). You should check them out."

"Yeah, you're right." Her mind races and she jumps in delight. "Hey, I know. We could do a music video or something. Create our own show with the class. Rico and Rosa could be in it too. With the horses."

Mr. Stryker gives a barking, skeptical laugh.

She looks at the theatre owner. "Sir, please don't blame Rico. I'm the one who brought a strange horse to your theatre. It's not his fault." She turns to the young horseman and fumbles with her backpack, unzips it, and reaches inside. "And Rico, I'm sorry I got you in trouble too. You were just trying to help me with Caesar." She carefully extracts the black silk hat from her bag. "Anyway, I saved this magic hat for you. It's the one I found in the carriage. The driver said it didn't belong to him. Maybe you could wear it in the horse shows. Or a music video." With a dramatic bow, she offers him the gleaming black hat, urging him to take it.

Rico self-consciously accepts the hat. "Gracias. But what's so magic about this hat?"

Suddenly aware of all the adults waiting for her answer, she feels a little foolish. "Well, uh, when you wear it, I think you can understand horses. I mean, at least I could understand Caesar. Especially when he was talking to Lady Pearl in her stall."

Mr. Stryker squints at her. His face grows pink as he clears his throat. Looking serious, he squats down to her level, straining his shabby corduroy trousers. "Listen, kiddo," he begins. His eyes dart toward her mother and he quickly adds, "Er, Maxzyne. I don't mind tellin' you that I can do without all the chaos in my stables and ring. Especially on a show night when I still gotta find someone to be Clara in *The Nutcracker* show since Maria's kid is sick." He pauses, looking pointedly at the watch on his hairy wrist then at the twins.

"B-b-but I really could understand him sometimes," Maxzyne stammers. "I mean, in a horse kind of way." She exhales and pulls her braids away from her face, afraid to look at her mother.

"Oh, Maxzyne. You and that imagination of yours. How many times does it land you in trouble?" Her mother sighs in exasperation.

Rico steps forward, spinning the fine hat by the brim. "Amiga, I'm not sure there is magic in this hat, but I know you have a heart for horses. *That's* why you can understand them. Maybe you are a Chicago-style gaucha. He looks at Rosa. "Like us, you lead with your heart." He smiles wide, his topaz eyes warm with admiration.

Maxzyne blushes and shrugs. *How can boys make you feel this fuzzy inside*? she wonders.

Mr. Stryker looks at Maxzyne. "Listen, if these twin gauchos keep up with their schoolwork and I can get more folks in the audience, your music video just might be possible. Deal?" He extends his bulky arm, enveloping her small hand in his beefy fingers.

"Deal," she echoes. "Does that also mean that you'll take care of Caesar?" she wheedles. "You'll adopt him, won't you? Rico says he used to be a show horse and should've never been on the streets pulling a carriage in the first place. Maybe you can use him in the show. After tonight, he's practically famous, right?"

19

Hearts without Fences

"M AXZYNE," HER FATHER WARNS. "Quit while you're ahead."

"But Dad," she cries plaintively. "You always say, 'If you're not the lead horse, the view never changes.' I'm just trying to make sure things change for the best. At least for Caesar anyway."

Her mother rolls her eyes. "Young lady, don't you dare use your own father's words against him. You can quote me: 'Respect your elders.' *We* decide what's best."

"Yes, but Mr. Stryker knows what's best for horses, right, sir?" Maxzyne gives him a pleading look.

Stryker looks at Officer Logan. "I assume the horse is being held at the police stables?"

The policeman nods. "He's in good hands at our South Shore stables for the moment. We'll see what the owner decides to do. By the time he pays his fines, he may decide to let the horse go. If that's the case," he turns to Rico, "He's all yours, young man."

"You say that horse has some potential, kid?" Stryker looks skeptical.

Rico considers the question and gives a vigorous nod. "Sí, señor. He is older but a good horse. Very smart. I think he just needs someone to listen to him. He could use a friend now."

"A gaucho friend," Maxzyne adds. "But it better be Rico." She shrugs, looking sheepish. "Because if it were me, I'd be doing all the talking." She flushes a bit when everyone around her laughs.

"¡Sí, sí! You are full of words," Rico agrees, his tan face breaking into a huge smile. "But your heart is as big as the pampas of our country. Open and wide. No fences." He looks at his sister. "Right, Rosa?" The other twin nods, her smile as dazzling as Rico's.

They even have matching dimples, Maxzyne marvels.

Stryker puts his hands on the heads of both twins. "So if we're done here, we've got a show to do."

Officer Logan waves at them all. "You're free to go. I'll get in touch about Caesar. Ace will keep him company tonight."

Stryker puts his plaid flannel cap back on his head and heads toward the command center entrance. "I've got to find someone who can fit into the Clara costume. There's no *Nutcracker* without Clara." The burly man jerks a thumb back at Maxzyne and her parents and adds, "Get a chance, come check out the show."

Stryker stops suddenly and turns around. "Wait a sec, you saw a bit of the show at practice, didn't you, young lady?" He squints Maxzyne, rubbing his bristly jaw with one calloused hand. "Just thinkin' out loud here and throwin' an idea out for consideration. Would you like to be Clara in the show tonight?"

Maxzyne's parents gasp. "Wha-aa-t?"

Rico and Rosa both clap their hands. "¡Sí! Do it. Be in the show with us just for tonight!"

20

"Community Service"

M-M-MEEE?" MAXZYNE STAMMERS. Her breath catches in her throat, making her cough. "You mean for real?" Astonished, she looks from her parents to the twins and back to Mr. Stryker. "Like, on stage?"

Rosa and Rico cover their mouths, unable to keep from giggling. "Not a stage. It's a ring, Maxzyne," Rosa corrects her.

Mr. Stryker nods. "Yeah. Just barely in the ring. Nothin' like these two." He cocks his head toward her parents. "It's a safe, easy role. You just have to pretend to like the nutcracker gift, go to sleep, and then wake up when he comes to life as your prince. You can pretend, can't you?"

Her mother laughs. "Oh, you have *no* idea how well she can pretend. Believe me, her imagination is vivid enough to keep me awake most nights." She looks at Maxzyne's father, who shakes his head and chuckles.

Maxzyne squeals in delight. "Of course I can pretend. I mean, I am the most awesome pretender in the universe." She whirls around to face Mr. Stryker again. "And there's even a costume I get to wear? How cool is that!" She grabs Rosa by both hands and swings them joyfully.

Mr. Stryker shrugs his shoulders and looks at her parents. "I'd be much obliged if you would let her do it just for tonight." He waggles his eyebrows at Officer Logan. "Maybe you could consider it 'community service,' Officer?"

"Please say I can do it, Mom and Dad." Dropping Rosa's hands, she clasps her palms together, pleading. "Please, please, please! I'll never, ever get in trouble again. Really. If you'll just grant me this one wish."

Her father winks at Officer Logan. "I've never seen someone go from possible jail time to horse theatre community service, have you, Officer?"

"Can't say I have, Mr. Merriweather," drawls the policeman. His lips curl upward and his eyes twinkle. "Ace and I would have to agree. Thought we'd seen it all, but this one's for the books."

Around her, everyone laughs. Maxzyne shrieks and hugs her parents. "Thank you, I love you!" She rocks back on her heels, holding her right hand over her heart. "And I promise I'll never, never, never, ever get in trouble again."

Hearing this, all the adults laugh. Maxzyne looks indignant. "Really!" she insists.

Mr. Stryker leans forward to shake her father's hand. Then he respectfully salutes her mother by raising his cap an inch or two off his forehead. Finally, he turns and corrals the three young people toward the command center entrance. "Okay, save the celebratin' for *after* the show. Let's hit the road, kids. Rico, you and Rosa go over the ropes with Maxzyne. Let her know the signals so she's on top of her act."

She whirls around to wave at her parents. "Mom? Dad? You're coming to the show, right?"

Mr. Stryker yells back as he ducks his head and shoulders through the command center entrance. "I'll have tickets waitin' for you at the box office, folks. See you ringside. You too, Officer."

Rico and Rosa quickly follow their boss outside. Maxzyne blows her parents a kiss just as Rico reaches back to grasp Maxzyne by the arm. He pulls her gently through the flap. "C'mon, Maxzyne. We've got a show to do."

She tumbles through the plastic sheet of the entrance, pausing to regain her balance. "Hey, just a sec. Rico, did you just call me Maxzyne?"

"Sí, señorita. Your mother expects respect. Do you think I am a *gaucho mal educado* (horseman without manners)? Hurry, we go!"

Boys. You think you have them figured out, and then you don't.

21

Stagestruck

INSIDE THE DARKENED THEATER, the buoyant strains of Tchaikovsky's *The Nutcracker Suite* fill the air. The audience quiets, settling into the rustic planked seats. A warm, buttery popcorn scent wafts through the air. This competes with the earthier aromas of horses, leather riding gear, and the performance ring's dirt.

In the shadowed center of the arena, Maxzyne waits for the show to begin. She is filled with nervous excitement and a tiny bit of anxiety, hoping she doesn't forget any of her part in the show. *Chillax. Breathe. Besides, it's a really small part. Nothing like Rico and Rosa's daredevil act on the horse.*

From the dark, she scans the crowd, hoping to see her parents. *Where are they? Shouldn't they be right in front?* Mr. Stryker assured her they would have great seats. *Wait! Is that Courtney Crowder in the second row? With all of the drill team from school?*

Maxzyne trains her eyes on the blonde troublemaker, watching the girls chatter together on their bench. She smiles to herself, imagining their surprise to see her in the show tonight. *They'll know it's me, right?* For once she's in the spotlight and not her rival. She remembers the sketch that Courtney took from her earlier. Maxzyne wants to blame her, but her conscience pricks. *I was just showing off. Trying to be cool, like her.* Her thoughts drift. Maybe now they have something in common. Who knows? They might be friends someday.

There is no time to find her parents in the crowd. The orchestra recording swells over the loudspeakers in the large open space. *Focus.* There is an expectant hush throughout the crowd as the lights slowly rise around her. In the center of the ring, an evergreen tree trimmed in old-fashioned glass ornaments appears through a misty haze. The crowd whistles, claps, and cheers.

Maxzyne, dressed as Clara, feels warm beneath the blue crushed-velvet cape with white faux-fur trim of her costume. Underneath, she wears a matching ankle-length dress and soft, tan leather booties that button up the sides. *Lights up. Showtime. Here goes.*

With a smile so wide it makes her cheeks hurt, she reaches to hang an ornament on a high branch of the shimmering tree. *Okay, ornament on tree. Check.* Once it is secured, she steps back to admire the tree, making the large taffeta bow in her hair flutter gently under the golden lights.

Right on cue, Fritz, her younger brother in the show, appears. He walks stiffly in a pair of old-fashioned satin breeches that come to his knees. His skinny legs below the knees are clad in tights and his black leather shoes feature large silver buckles. His costume is topped off by a striped jacket and white ruffled shirt. As he takes his place by the tree, he looks at her and smirks. She learned earlier, when she met Maria's younger brother, that he hates to play this part in the show. He'd rather be one of the clowns on horseback.

She watches as he rises on his toes in those clunky shoes, the glass bird ornament wobbling in his hand. *Is he gonna drop it?* she wonders. At last he manages to hang his glass ornament even higher than hers. He sticks his tongue out at her. It doesn't take much pretending or acting after that. The two compete with each other, both trying to reach the highest branch. *Gee, maybe I'm glad I don't have a little brother. What a pest.*

Suddenly, the music changes, reflecting the arrival of her godfather, Herr Drosselmeyer. The roving spotlight follows the slim, dark-haired man as he enters the ring. He wears his hair in a long ponytail and his gray silk jacket is trimmed in oversized sterling buttons. He cuts quite a figure as he proudly rides a black stallion whose glossy dark mane and tail are trimmed in red and gold silk tassels.

Despite the costume, Maxzyne recognizes Rico and Rosa's father, Señor Callea. She also knows that he's riding Ajax, whose mane and tail were sprayed and brushed to a lustrous shine using a mixture of Listerine, baby oil, and water.

I love community service, she marvels. *I'm learning so much cool stuff.* She is relieved to know that the Callea family is able to continue working at the theater. Señora Callea, the twins' mother, introduced herself to Maxzyne backstage earlier. She even thanked her for helping get Rico and Rosa more interested in school with her proposed video that will feature the twins' horsemanship and favorite Uruguayan music.

Maxzyne and Fritz rush to greet Drosselmeyer as he stops to admire the Christmas tree and its decorations. Reaching into his saddlebag, the man retrieves two gifts: a wooden nutcracker for Clara and a riding stick for her brother. Both act excited to accept the gifts. As Drosselmeyer watches, Clara dances around the tree with the precious nutcracker in her arms. Fritz rides his pretend horse, running fast and chasing Clara.

Uh, oh! Almost forgot to loosen the latch on the doll's neck. As she runs, Maxzyne pops it open with her thumbnail, like Rosa showed her earlier. Just in time, because seconds later, Fritz knocks the nutcracker from her arms. Her empty hands fly to her face. She pretends to be sad when the head falls off the body and lands on the ground. As she kneels down to pick up both pieces of the doll, Drosselmeyer shakes his finger at Fritz. However, the scolding is interrupted when a clock chimes. Maxzyne carefully places the broken nutcracker under the Christmas tree and the two siblings are sent away to bed.

Whew. So far, so good. No mistakes. At least not yet. Maxzyne settles down on her make-believe bed in a darkened corner of the ring. Pretending to sleep, she nearly closes her eyes, but the sound of a familiar laugh makes her turn to look at the crowd. Sure enough, several yards to the right, her parents sit on a long bench. Her father offers a bag of popcorn to—*Say what? Is that Principal Farwell? Wait a sec.* She blinks twice, to be sure. *No way. And that's Miss Garrett too. Yikes.* Feeling nervous and a little self-conscious, she lays her head back down on the satin pillow. *Well, I sure hope they know this is part of my community service.*

The music softens, the lights glow, and there is a hint of magic in the air. Maxzyne closes her eyes, waiting for the clock to strike midnight so the nutcracker under the tree can come to life. She feels drowsy and fights to stay awake. *This show biz stuff is kinda fun. Hmm . . . who knows? Maybe I'll be an actress when I grow up!*

Acknowledgments

A S MUCH AS I WOULD LIKE TO THINK that I created this book by simply sitting alone at the keyboard and marshaling my daydreams onto these pages, it would not be the case. Every author knows that it takes a team to make a book, and I have a wonderful team that I think of as "TEAM MAXZYNE." It is my good fortune that this team includes some great friends.

To keep me from straying off the story path, I must give full credit to my developmental editor, Jill Welsh. She is a firm and patient guiding light when it comes to staying true to the brand and tale, despite my inclination to wander. Copy editor and book production manager Kim Bookless is another team member who is vital to the publishing process. She easily explains the nuts and bolts of every thorny issue that arises when I get confused or forget the details. She gives her best to every page and can spot an error quicker than a hawk hunting a squirrel lunch. For the *español*, I was fortunate to have Jennifer Murtoff give the dialogue an authentic and accurate portrayal of the Callea family. Book Discussion and Activity Guide creator Elizabeth Riedel put her analytical skills to work and teased out the best parts of the story for young readers to identify and discuss. Her crossword puzzle and word game are both fun and educational activities. I must also thank my mentor and teacher, Cheryl Coons, for her many lessons in finding and telling a good story. Her valuable insights gave me the confidence to write and the tools to create a compelling tale. Finally, I am thrilled that my niece Rebecca Robinson is able to share her illustration skills in this book. Just like Maxzyne, she knows that no matter what your age, you can make a difference.

Book Discussion Guide

by Elizabeth Riedel

Chapter 1: The Sketch of Doom

Why is Maxzyne sent to the principal's office? Do you agree with her reasoning that "No way it's my fault!" Do you think she did anything wrong?

Why did she draw the picture in the first place? And why did she show it to Courtney?

Maxzyne gets caught by the teacher in part because she put her name on the drawing. Why does an artist or craftsperson put his or her name on a creation?

Her parents make her memorize a big vocabulary word as punishment when she has done something wrong. Is that a fair punishment? Why or why not?

Maxzyne does not care for folksy songs. Why would the music teacher have chosen such music for the class?

Chapter 2: Caesar

Why didn't Maxzyne go straight to the principal's office?

Was her decision to go outside without telling anyone a smart choice? What other options did she have?

What does she encourage Caesar to do after she frees the carriage wheel from the bike rack?

Why does she climb into the carriage? Do you think she realized there was the possibility that the horse would run down the street away from the school?

Chapter 3: Rico and Rosa

The carriage drivers use horses to drive tourists around to earn a living. What do you think of animals being use by humans to earn money? Can it be done fairly and humanely?

Who should set the rules governing the use of animals as laborers? Businesspeople? Farm workers? Animal rights advocates? Schoolchildren?

What punishment should people get for breaking the rules protecting animals?

Rico and Maxzyne get off to a bad start. He first accuses her of mistreating the horse and later accuses her of stealing it. She considers him strange and rude and calls him a know-it-all. Why do you think there is tension between them?

Rico unfairly assumed that Maxzyne was the owner of the horse and yelled at her for mistreating the animal. Think of an example of when you jumped to a conclusion (or made an assumption) but were wrong. What would you do differently the next time? What can happen when you make false assumptions about people and their motives? How does it feel when they make false assumptions about you?

When Maxzyne pretends she and Rico are taking Caesar on the freight elevator in her condo, the tension between the two of them starts to ease. Can you think of a time when humor helped to calm down a tense situation?

Why do you think Maxzyne was reluctant at first to accept Rico's offer to help find the horse's owner? Do you think she could have saved the horse by herself? Do you think she wanted to?

Who comes up with a plan on how to save the horse? How do Maxzyne and Rico (after bickering) decide to work together to find the horse's owner?

Why do you think Rosa calls Rico *hermanito* (little brother) when they are actually twins?

Maxzyne agrees to hide under the carriage in the stable while Rico and Rosa go to practice their act. Should she have waited under the tarp for Rico to return? What choices did she have then?

Chapter 4: The Old Horse Theatre

Maxzyne wonders how Rico and Rosa can have a job even though they are children. Do you think children should be allowed to work? Under what circumstances would it be okay or not okay?

Maxzyne can understand what Caesar and Lady Pearl are saying to each other when she wears the magic hat. Can you communicate with your pet? How do they communicate with you?

Do you think animals can communicate with each other, like Caesar and Lady Pearl? Can they have relationships or friendships with each other? What does that tell us about their nature?

Mr. Stryker gives directions to Rico and Rosa as they practice their act. How would you describe him as a boss? Is it fair for him to ask them to put up flyers to advertise the show in addition to the work they do as performers?

Chapter 5: Rico to the Rescue

Why do you think Rico is so skilled with horses?

Why is Mr. Stryker mad at Rico and Maxzyne for bring Caesar to the stable? Is his anger fair or unfair? How does he treat Rico and his family?

What motivated Rico to rescue Caesar out of the stable? Did he consider Rosa's warning that they might lose their jobs if they crossed Mr. Stryker? What was the most important factor for him? Do you agree with his reasoning?

Chapter 6: Trust

Rico and Rosa go to school in the morning in a "newcomer" program, but some children call it the "dummy" program. Why would they call it that? Is it fair to the newcomers?

Rico is reluctant to go to Maxzyne's friend Officer Logan for help. She explains that she trusts him and encourages Rico to trust other people sometimes. Why is Rico afraid of the police? Why doesn't he want to engage with the police?

Rico describes his experience crossing the border into the United States. What do you think about his experience? How do you think our country should treat people who are coming here to live and work?

Maxzyne tells Rico that it is pretty special to have a twin like Rosa and always be part of a team. Do you ever wish you had a twin? Could a best friend be as special and close to you as a natural-born twin?

Chapter 7: Officer Logan

Do you think Officer Logan is knowledgeable about horses?

What type of horse does Officer Logan say are able to be out on the streets?

What does Officer Logan notice about Caesar?

Chapter 8: Plan B

After Office Logan announces that the horse is stolen, Maxzyne runs away on Caesar. Why did she do that? What else could she have done?

Rico always carries a scarf/bandana that his grandmother made for him. She said it would protect him and his horse. Do you think it's true that it could protect him? Do you have an object that is special to you? Why is it special? How does it make you feel when you hold it?

Maxzyne mentions an "outside-the-box plan." What does that mean?

Maxzyne aspires to save not just Caesar but every horse in the city. What is the compromise solution she offers to please horse owners, the horses, and the public? Do you think you have the ability to make change where you live? Is there something you would like to change?

Chapter 9: Jerry the Balloon Man

How does Jerry the balloon man assist Maxzyne while she is on Michigan Avenue in the parade crowd? Do you think he made a wise decision?

Chapter 10: Stop, Thief!

Maxzyne admits to Jerry that she freaked after she learned the horse was reported stolen. As she does, her shoulders are shaking. But she realizes that admitting to a grown-up that she contributed to her current problems makes her feel a bit better. How can owning up to a problem make a person feel better?

Chapter 11: Plan C

Maxzyne's father says, "Success is going from failure to failure without losing enthusiasm." She realizes Plan B didn't work but doesn't give up. She thinks hard and comes up with another plan that is not revealed until later chapters. Have you ever felt stuck trying to figure out a solution to a problem? What helped you eventually solve the problem?

Chapter 12: Taking a Stand

As Maxzyne makes her way through the crowd, wondering how she will help Rico and Caesar, she thinks that being only eleven years old could actually help her situation/cause. How does being only an eleven-year-old benefit her?

Maxzyne thinks that it must be hard to be a politician, especially when folks don't like what you say or do. What do you think it's like to be a politician? Would you like to be one someday?

Chapter 13: Compromise

Maxzyne insists that the council say the Pledge of Allegiance before they start their impromptu council meeting. What does the pledge mean for our country? Why do we say it? What does it mean to you?

An Iraq war veteran steps forward from the crowd, carrying a small American flag and a copy of the US Constitution. Why do you think he carries it with him at all times?

The city council discusses penalties for anyone caught violating the rule about how animals are treated. Is the threat of punishment enough to stop someone from doing something wrong?

The carriage drivers make their case for why they want to continue taking tourists around on the city streets.

Maxzyne realizes there are two sides to every story and wonders why anyone would want to be a lawyer. She worries about how they would feel if they made a wrong choice or a bad rule. Do you usually recognize that a story has two sides? Would you feel comfortable with the responsibility that lawyers or council members have of possibly making a wrong choice or bad rule?

Chapter 14: Whose Hat?

The crowd recognizes Maxzyne as the girl who got the vote for city carriage horses when the police escort her away. *"Who would think that someone so young could accomplish that?"* What do you think the young can accomplish? Do you know any examples of young people making noteworthy accomplishments?

Chapter 15: Command Center

Rosa concludes that Mr. Stryker, her brother, and she all need each other to make the show a success. What is your experience in working on a team? Can you think of examples of something you couldn't accomplish by yourself but could as part of a team?

At the police station, Maxzyne sketches a horse and young rider that makes her "forget everything" except her drawing. She realizes that her sketch of the music teacher got her into trouble at school that day and thinks her drawing is *"the best and worst part of me."* Do you think an activity can help people to forget everything? Do you have such an activity? How could it be both the best and worst part of a person?

Chapter 16: Officer Logan's Discovery

How did the commotion on Michigan Avenue help bring a bigger audience to the horse theatre performance that evening?

Chapter 17: The Dreaded Sketch

Maxzyne apologizes to Mr. Stryker for all the trouble she has caused. She offers to help with the horses even though she doesn't know much about them, promising that she can learn. She also offers her drawing skills to help the show. In what ways could you help someone, or a cause, even if you don't have specific skills normally associated with the task?

Chapter 18: Getting in Harmony

Maxzyne admits that she was mad at the other students after her sketch of Miss Garrett went viral, but she realizes she also should have been mad at herself. Officer Logan understands and says that many people end up in trouble with the law because they blame everyone else but themselves. Why is it important to look at your actions and take responsibility for them?

What lesson does Maxzyne learn about the importance of having rules? She admits she hates having them. What do you think about rules at school, for horses, for people? Do you think they are necessary?

Maxzyne defends Rico to an angry Mr. Stryker and apologizes to Rico for getting him into trouble. She decides to give Rico the magic black silk hat. Why do you think she does so?

Chapters 19 through 22:

Maxzyne talks about how much she loves community service and how much cool stuff she has learned. Do you have any experience in community service? What did you learn?

General Questions:

How would you describe Maxzyne to a friend of yours? What qualities about her do you admire? What advice would you give her if you met her?

How would you describe Rico? What qualities do you admire and what advice would you give him?

Throughout the book, Maxzyne gives commentary about boys. For example, at the end of Chapter 6, she thinks: *Geez! Boys should come with a warning: Will make fun of anything a girl says or does at all times.* Did you agree with her commentary?

Maxzyne often quotes advice from her father. What do you think of her father's wisdom? Are his sayings helpful?

Science says smell is the most powerful sense to evoke memories, and the book often describes a scene with language about smells. For example, at the end of the book, in the Old Horse Theatre "a warm, buttery popcorn scent" wafted through the air. Do you recall any of these descriptions? Which ones did you relate to?

What did Maxzyne learn from the whole adventure?

Discuss what you like about the book. What would you say in a letter to the author? What other types of adventures do you envision for Maxzyne?

Maxzyne and the Old Horse Theatre

Elizabeth Riedel

EclipseCrossword.com

Across

4. famous tower on Michigan Avenue
6. favored food of horses
8. snack that twins at parade share with Maxzyne
9. Maxzyne's role in *The Nutcracker*
11. skilled horseman (in Spanish)
13. highest elected official of a city
15. Maxzyne's last name
17. carriage riders
18. doctor who could speak to animals

Down

1. Maxzyne's favored carryall
2. special place for Maxzyne, Rico, Caesar, and others
3. main avenue in Chicago
5. Jerry's specialty
7. Caesar's lady friend
10. type of circumstance that got Maxzyne sent to the principals office
12. one of Maxzyne's favorite desserts
14. Maxzyne's go-to hairstyle

Maxzyne and the Old Horse Theatre

Elizabeth Riedel

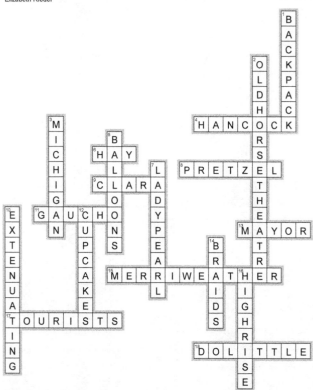

EclipseCrossword.com

Spanish and English Vocabulary
Match *Spanish* and English words from the two columns. The first answer is provided.

1) *amigo* **(answer: d)**

2) *De nada*

3) *Esta bien*

4) *jefe*

5) *sí*

6) *carros*

7) *autobuses*

8) *motocicletas*

9) *ambulancias*

10) *dinero*

11) *turistas*

12) *loco*

13) *todo el tiempo*

14) *caballo*

15) *las raices*

16) *hermanito*

17) *rapido*

18) *relájate*

19) *El Capitán*

20) *¡Basta, ya!*

a) yes

b) little brother

c) boss

d) friend

e) roots

f) horse

g) That's good

h) tourists

i) It's nothing

j) cars

k) The Captain

l) ambulance

m) relax

n) Whoa!

o) motorcycles

p) buses

q) money

r) fast

s) all the time

t) crazy

About the Author

Photo by Laura Robinson

CAROLINE LEE lives in Delray Beach, Florida, where she is busy making friends and dreaming up new adventures for Maxzyne. While there are many opportunities to swim in the ocean, she prefers to walk along the beach and admire the sunsets with her husband, Rebel.

About the Illustrator

Illustrator Rebecca Robinson lives in Knoxville, Tennessee, where she spends all her free time doodling on math homework and writing songs on her guitar. She loves going on adventures, visiting her aunt, and eating way too much chocolate!

*If you liked this book,
read another Maxzyne adventure!*

It's a race against the clock when a wayward freight elevator, a family of enchanted vintage mannequins in distress, and a secret tunnel propel Maxzyne Merriweather straight into the mysterious depths of a historic Chicago department store. Can the impulsive heroine save her new mannequin friends before it's too late?

www.maxzyne.com

CPSIA information can be obtained
at www.ICGtesting.com
Printed in the USA
FSHW011811150220

9 780990 661733